*W*hat the critics are saying...

ℬ

"Weredemons, secret agents, and spicy hot sex are all prime ingredients in *Denise A. Agnew's IMPETUOUS...* *Denise* continues her mind-gripping Special Investigations Agency series with another page-turner. *IMPETUOUS* has paranormal elements, suspense, and sexual tension in spades, all woven together into a tale that leaves readers clamoring for more." ~ *Sinclair Reid Romance Reviews Today*

"...a fascinating story involving suspense, the paranormal and hot spicy erotic romance. It is part of the Special Investigation Agency Series but the book stands alone...This is a delightful and entertaining book with a wonderful ending. The strength of the character's love and their devotion will bring tears to your eyes. Add Impetuous to your bookshelf!" ~ *Julie Esparza Just Erotic Romance Reviews*

"The passion between Synna and Ian lights up the pages and the sex scenes are very sensuous and hot...There are some unexpected twists in the story that keeps it fresh and interesting. *IMPETUOUS* is defiantly not one to miss!" ~ *Julia, Romance Reviews Today*

"Oh man, I couldn't put this book down....If you have not read this book yet, go to get it, you will not be sorry." ~ Nicole, *Enchanted In Romance*

"The heat from the chemistry between Synna and Ian warms your entire body. The story is a page turner where things are not always as they seem. *Ms. Agnew* has written another wonderful installment in her SIA series." ~ *Cindy Warner Karen Find Out About New Books Coffee Time Romance*

"What a terrific book. I have read nearly all of *Denise A. Agnew's* SIA books, but this one is my favorite. The plot is so well written and really suspenseful with a surprise at the end of the book. Another keeper..." ~ *Danny, Cupid's Library Reviews*

"*IMPETUOUS* is the newest installment in *Ms. Agnew's* Special Investigation Agency series and it's every bit as good as the other ones! The Special Investigation Series is definitely one of my all time favorite series - they are the kinds of books I'd buy without having to read a summary of the story, because I just know I will fall in love with the characters...*IMPETUOUS* convinces with clever plotting, wicked ideas as well as a great show-down at the end of the story...As always with this author's books, I never want them to end." ~ *Frauke, Cupid's Library Reviews*

Impetuous

DENISE A. AGNEW

ELLORA'S CAVE
ROMANTICA PUBLISHING

An Ellora's Cave Romantica Publication

www.ellorascave.com

Impetuous

ISBN # 1419952692
ALL RIGHTS RESERVED.
Impetuous Copyright © 2005 Denise A. Agnew
Edited by Martha Punches
Cover art by Syneca

Electronic book Publication April 2005
Trade paperback Publication October 2005

Warning:

The following material contains graphic sexual content meant for mature readers. *Impetuous* has been rated *E-rotic* by a minimum of three independent reviewers.

Ellora's Cave Publishing offers three levels of Romantica™ reading entertainment: S (S-ensuous), E (E-rotic), and X (X-treme).

S-*ensuous* love scenes are explicit and leave nothing to the imagination.

E-*rotic* love scenes are explicit, leave nothing to the imagination, and are high in volume per the overall word count. In addition, some E-rated titles might contain fantasy material that some readers find objectionable, such as bondage, submission, same sex encounters, forced seductions, etc. E-rated titles are the most graphic titles we carry; it is common, for instance, for an author to use words such as "fucking", "cock", "pussy", etc., within their work of literature.

X-*treme* titles differ from E-rated titles only in plot premise and storyline execution. Unlike E-rated titles, stories designated with the letter X tend to contain controversial subject matter not for the faint of heart.

Also by Denise A. Agnew

୧୭

By Honor Bound *(anthology)*
The Dare
Deep is the Night: Dark Fire
Deep is the Night: Haunted Souls
Deep is the Night: Night Watch
Ellora's Cavemen: Tales From the Temple IV *(anthology)*
Special Investigations Agency: Over the Line
Special Investigations Agency: Primordial
Winter Warriors *(anthology)*
Special Investigation: Sins and Secrets
Men to Die For

Impetuous
Special Investigations Agency
ɷ

Dedication

ᔍ

As always, for the love of my life, Terry.

Trademarks Acknowledgement

The author acknowledges the trademarked status and trademark owners of the following wordmarks mentioned in this work of fiction:

Aragorn and The Lord of the Rings: Property of the estate of JRR Tolkien.

Chapter One
Special Investigations Agency
Location: Top Secret, somewhere in Colorado

ဢ

"Perhaps you should just do him."

Over the din of the crowded cafeteria, Synna MacDell stared at her new coworker Heidi Swearengen in disbelief. "What? Who?"

"You know who I mean." Heidi winked. "Every day since I started here, it's been the same thing."

Puzzled, Synna took a sip of her decaf coffee to stall for time. "I don't have a clue what you're talking about."

Heidi's toss of long, black ringlets and cocoa skin reminded Synna of an African American Shirley Temple. Cute and sometimes perky to the point of nails-over-the-blackboard irritation, Heidi had the reputation of nosy busybody, and she'd been in this new position less than a week. She'd transferred from another division where she'd worked for several months. Generous cleavage and ample hips, plus a plucky attitude seemed to attract men to Heidi like starving hogs to a trough. Men in Division Two made a point of stopping by the cubicle far more often than they did when Synna had been there alone.

Heidi smirked. "We hit the cafeteria after training and less than a half hour this tall, blond Adonis goes by and you stare at him like he's chocolate. It's not a passing look either. More of a hot, greet 'em and eat 'em."

A deep blush swept into Synna's face and she shoved away her almost finished salad. Since she'd agreed to train her replacement at Division Two, she'd spent time in the cafeteria at lunch. Usually she ate a brown-bag lunch, but Heidi said she hated to make lunch and wanted to eat in the cafeteria every day. Conceding to the stubborn woman's wishes eroded Synna's hard-won confidence. She knew better than to let pushy individuals control her actions. Add this to Heidi's obsession with Synna's lack of love life and Synna had about enough. She'd let things get out of control and needed to salvage what she could.

"Ah, come on." Heidi leaned over the round table, her cloying perfume wafting under Synna's nose. "You're blushing. You know what I'm talking about. He's due to walk in any moment."

Oh yeah. Synna knew who she meant all right. Every woman at Special Investigations Agency knew the Big Kahuna. The Boss. Da Man. All women with half a hormone left recognized former soldier Ian Frasier. The youngest man to become head of SIA, the thirty-six-year-old Frasier started the job about a month ago. In that time, he'd single-handedly conquered the hearts and minds of females from Division One all the way up to Level Ten.

"Mr. Frasier is good-looking." Synna shrugged. "So what?"

"Pfft! He's more than good-looking. He's gorgeous and has a great personality, from what I hear."

"He probably has a significant other or twenty women after him all at one time. I don't think I'd like the competition."

Heidi snorted softly. "Come on, girl. Where is your sense of adventure?"

Good question. Buried under work most of the time, she'd allowed life to morph into dreary routine over the last year. She knew it was nobody's fault but hers. She needed to resurrect her social life and break the pattern. Her first move meant leaving the SIA to pursue what she'd wanted to do all her life. Two more weeks and she'd be dust in the wind. Gone. Out of here.

"Wait a minute. There's Tyler. You could always take him as a second choice," Heidi said.

Synna's gaze swung to Tyler Hessler moving toward them from across the room. While tall, dark and good-looking, he did nothing for her gonads. In fact, he drove her to within an inch of screaming. He strode up, his grin wide and almost boyish. He wore an attractive navy blue sweater and dark cords. Although thin as a giraffe, his male beauty showed in rumpled cappuccino hair and finely cut features. He just didn't do diddly for her.

Unfortunately, she did something for him. He'd hounded her for three weeks asking for a date, and his unrelenting attention made her more nervous by the day. He didn't know when to quit.

She plastered on a pleasant smile and greeted him. He shuffled his feet like an embarrassed schoolboy. Heidi grinned, but her friendliness ended there. The woman's gaze scanned the crowd of lunching employees as if she scouted for a more tasty meal. Synna wanted to brain Heidi with something heavy. Preferably with a long and boring regulation manual.

"Excuse me," Heidi said as she stood up and took her tray. "I need to get rid of this. Be back in a minute."

Tyler slid into an empty chair across from Synna. "I'm glad I caught you."

I'll just bet you are.

"You know the Halloween party that Mr. Frasier is having Friday night? Do you have a date for it?"

Oh boy. "Um…I'm not going with a date, Tyler. I'm going alone."

A flicker of self-consciousness darted through his olive green eyes. "Go with me. I've got this cutting-edge pirate costume. What are you wearing?"

She spilled the beans before she could stop herself. "A serving wench."

She'd been uncertain about the daring costume at first, aware that her cleavage would be well-exposed.

His eyes danced with appreciation. "Hey, that sounds sexy."

She took a deep breath. "I'm going alone, Tyler. I'm not taking a date."

He shrugged, clear disappointment reflected in his frown. "No problem. I can take the hint."

She didn't like being mean to him, but she'd turned him down three times. Before she could speak, he shoved his chair back and left without a word. He'd taken her other rejections with more good-hearted understanding. Now he looked pissed off. What could she do? Nothing. Something about him made her uneasy. She couldn't define it but the feeling stayed with her.

Heidi returned less than three minutes later. She plopped back in the chair. "Thank goodness. I'm sorry I left you like that, but he annoys me." Heidi perked up and then patted her hair. "Oh my God. Now there's a *real* man."

Ian Frasier strolled into the cafeteria. Synna glanced at the clock on the wall. Yes. Twelve-thirty to be exact.

Over six feet tall, with a distinctive stride that spelled confidence, Ian Frasier didn't look like a soldier. His thick, wavy champagne blond hair grew down to touch his shoulders. Some days he wore his hair pulled back. Today he'd left it loose.

His dress code was more relaxed than the former head of the premier intelligence agency. Sweaters and dress pants, rather than suits, ruled the day. Today he wore a Fair Isle burgundy sweater and dark blue pants that fit him as if tailored. Since the first day she'd seen him, Synna admired his slim but powerful body. Broad shoulders, strong arms and flat stomach defined most of the male agents at SIA because of physical fitness requirements. With Ian, she felt something different when she looked at him. Her pulse fluttered and her heart skipped beats.

Heidi's voice went down to a low purr. "What I wouldn't do to try that man on for size. He looks like he knows what he's doing when it comes to sex."

Synna resisted the temptation to kick Heidi under the table. "How can you tell by looking at him?"

Heidi laughed. "Girl, I just know."

Ian bypassed the cafeteria line where he often picked up a salad or sandwich and then left. Instead, his gaze found Synna and Heidi and he headed right for them.

"He's coming this way," Synna said, a little out of breath.

Heidi went silent, much to Synna's surprise. No time to prepare, no time to primp or arrange anything witty to say. Ian stopped at their table. His eyes sparkled like clear, cold lake waters, but with a heat and intent Synna found arousing.

He caught her gaze for a heart-stopping moment and his smile held so much warmth and friendliness she couldn't think straight. She realized he always looked at her like this. Whenever he had popped into Division Two and said hello, his azure eyes twinkled and a roguish smile curved those well-carved lips. His attention made her feel extraordinary. As if he just might feel an attraction to her, too.

The critic on her shoulder snorted with disdain. *Who are you kidding? He's friendly to everyone. The way he looks at you isn't special. Get over it.*

"Afternoon, Synna. Heidi. How are you?" His voice, whisky-potent and satin-rich, was deep and intoxicating.

"I'm fine." Synna kept her voice pitched evenly, though her stomach filled with annoying butterflies. Her pulse started a frantic pace.

Before Synna could say more, Heidi broke in.

"I'm wonderful." Heidi's toothy smile went so wide it looked like she might stretch her face out of shape. "How are you, Mr. Frasier?"

He crossed his arms. "Never been better. Are you ready for the Halloween party coming up?"

Heidi tossed her hair back. "I'm *so* ready. I'm considering wearing a mask."

"I can't wear a mask. People will get nervous if they think the boss is lurking around incognito," he said.

She admired how nothing seemed to faze him. Not conflict, not concern. She often wondered, as she went to sleep at night, what the real Ian Frasier would be like one-on-one. Would he reveal deeper sides to him? Darker nuances she wouldn't admire so much? The idea of finding out was both petrifying and delicious.

"My costume is easy. A-a serving wench," she said without thinking. Another flush headed her face. *God, that sounded lame as hell.*

She hated to stutter, and although she didn't do it often anymore, it happened in moments of sheer confusion or if she became flustered.

He laughed, but instead of creating embarrassment inside her, the genuine humor and appreciation in his gaze made her feel welcome. A part of the joke, not the butt of it. "Glad to hear you're going to be there. Well, ladies, I've got to go. See you later."

He took off without another word, and Synna admired him as he moved away.

"I can't believe you didn't flirt with him." Heidi sat back in her hard plastic chair. "Unless it was me he wanted to see."

Disgusted and weary, Synna stood and picked up her tray. She made sure to keep her voice pitched low. She didn't want anyone else to hear her. "I'm not going to flirt with the head of this organization. I have paperwork to do before the day is over. Enjoy the rest of your lunch break."

She tried to smile, but it didn't work. She'd worn her glee muscles down to a nub this week. Heidi's puzzled look almost made her regret her stern words.

Her tone must have made an impression, because when Heidi came back to the cubicle from lunch, she seemed a little more subdued. The afternoon wore on with Synna showing Heidi more details of the job. Heidi seemed competent to perform the work, and Synna didn't feel bad about leaving her position to someone who could handle the complicated filing system, the computer and various other administrative tasks. Heidi left right before five o'clock, but Synna stayed. She often remained late to finish tasks better completed without noise and human activity breaking her concentration. God, how nice it would be to finally have time for her art, for the career she'd wanted forever.

She finished filling a box with mementos from her almost ten years at SIA. Pictures of past employees who hadn't lasted as long at SIA. Birthday cards from coworkers. Her family photographs would go with her on her last day.

The last day. She felt sad whenever she thought of it. Like a child afraid to go to bed at night and therefore miss anything the grown-ups might experience, part of her felt bereft. Deep silence pervaded the cubicles in the large administration area and echoed in her heart. She also felt a little empty. Was she making a mistake leaving SIA? Tonight she'd go home to her quiet condo and think about it, but the damage had been done. She'd turned in her resignation over eight weeks ago.

She analyzed why her emotions were so untidy. The last week had been tough, but leaving SIA to pursue her dreams must be the right course of action. Tears stung her eyes and escaped before she could stop them. She wiped away the moisture with her fingers.

A sound behind her made her start and whirl around.

The last person in the world she expected to see stood at the entrance to her cubicle.

"Tyler."

He moved into the cubicle, his cheesy grin diminishing his handsomeness. "What are you doing here so late?"

"I'm doing some last-minute work. What about you?"

He edged into her personal space. "I was making my way across the offices when I saw you standing there. You look like you need a friend."

No, no, no. Hasn't he given up yet?

Synna managed to plaster on a semblance of a smile. "I'm good. Thanks for checking on me."

"Heidi said you might need some bucking up. That you're depressed about leaving the SIA."

Indignation rose inside her, but she kept her expression controlled. "S-she's very mistaken. I'm looking forward to my career change."

His sickly sweet cologne made her want to back away, not to mention his unwanted proximity. His interested gaze blazed down at her, but she couldn't feel one tingle of response.

"I know you said you didn't want to go out, but—"

"No," she said. "I don't, Tyler. When I say no, I mean no."

If the man had personality to go with his looks, she would have found him attractive. As it was, his insistent bugging made her want to break his kneecaps.

He clasped her shoulders and yanked her up against him. "I don't think you mean that."

Before she could blink, his mouth came down on hers.

Chapter Two

೫೦

Hot and messy, Tyler's lips sipped at hers. Recoiling, Synna pushed at his chest, her protest muffled against his mouth.

She shoved harder and he released her abruptly. She stumbled and her knee cracked against the sharp corner of a small table near her desk. Pain rocketed through her, and she yelped. Tears surged into her eyes at the stabbing sensation, and she clutched at her knee and sat down quickly in her chair.

"Damn it. Tyler, what the hell do you think you're doing?"

His eyebrows drew together, but he didn't look sorry. "Well, if you hadn't backed away so fast this wouldn't have happened."

Trembling with reaction, she pointed toward the cubicle exit. "Please get out."

"If it's because you're a supervisor, don't worry about it. You're leaving SIA and we can—"

"Synna said she wants you to leave," Ian's deep, commanding voice came from behind Tyler. "If I was you, I'd do it."

Tyler jumped and turned around as Ian walked into the cubicle. "Oh, Mr...uh...sorry, Mr. Frasier. I didn't see you."

Ian looked mad enough to chew uncooked yak meat. "Apparently not."

Tyler's chest puffed out, as if he planned to be stupid enough to challenge the most powerful man in SIA.

Oh my God. The weasel wants to take on the head of SIA? Is he out of his mind?

"We were just talking," Tyler said a hint of defiance in his tone.

Ian's stance, arms akimbo and feet braced apart, held a distinctive ready-to-rumble quality, overlaid by a veneer of civilization. "It looked to me like you were kissing her against her will."

Tyler glared. "No, you see, we've been going out."

"What?" Anger rose up inside her. Irritation brought more tears to her eyes, and she took a shuddering breath. "We are *not*."

Tyler's nervous grin went with his thin voice as he said, "She's just angry with me."

Synna took a deep breath to force the quaver out of her voice. "I'm more than angry, Tyler. Please don't ever talk to me again."

"But—"

"Hessler." Ian's frown went deeper. "You need to get out of here right now before I lose my professionalism."

Leashed power vibrated from Ian. His eyes seemed to have darkened, and the menace etched into his features said he could be dangerous if the situation warranted. As if he might consider arguing a little more, Tyler didn't move. While he'd always been annoying, she never suspected he could be this dim-witted.

Tyler threw them both a hateful look then left the cubicle.

Ian's features calmed and instantly turned into a worried frown. He squatted down in front of her. His eyes held hers, concentrated with genuine concern that warmed her. This close, the rugged lines of his face became clear. His jawline held determination, and his Roman nose sported a slight crookedness that prevented it from being too perfect. His eyebrows were a little darker than his hair, and thick golden lashes framed the most remarkable eyes she'd seen.

She drew in his intoxicating scent, a cross between soft sandalwood and musk. God, he smelled so good, she could drown in everything unique and gorgeous about him.

"Did he hurt you?" he asked.

She shook her head and rubbed her knee. "N-no. Nothing but my pride."

His glance fell to her knee. "I heard you cry out. What's wrong with your knee?"

"When he let me go I hit it on the corner of that table."

He winced. "Damn, that must have hurt like hell."

"It did."

"How does it feel now?"

"A little sore, but I think it'll be fine."

A gentle smile touched his mouth. "If it isn't, make sure to stop by medical before you leave tonight, okay?"

A feeling of total safety cradled her. "Will do."

"What's going on between you and Tyler?"

She didn't want to explain the awkward situation, but she couldn't hide it from him either. "He's been hounding me for a date for three weeks. I've said no, but he doesn't listen."

His frown deepened. "Is he stalking you?"

Startled, she shook her head. "Really, I hadn't thought of it as stalking. I mean, he seems harmless enough."

"He's not harmless, Synna, if he was willing to force himself on you. Then when you hurt yourself, he wasn't concerned about it. There's something wrong there."

She couldn't disagree. "I'll keep a watch on it, and if it gets worse, I'll tell human resources."

He stood up slowly. "Good."

"B-but—" She cut herself off.

One of his eyebrows twitched upward in question. "But?"

She shook her head as more tears moistened her eyes. She couldn't remember the last time she'd felt so unable to control her emotions. The damned stuttering had returned without remorse. "N-nothing. I just didn't want to go out on a note like this."

"What he did isn't your fault." His features hardened, his disagreement edged in deep lines. A gentle grin erased the harshness on his face. "Your judge of character is pretty damned good. You rejected him before and it was for a good reason." Ian's understanding took her off-guard, but he didn't give her a chance to acknowledge it. "How does the knee feel now?"

"Much better." His closeness and eagerness to comfort touched a tender spot deep in her heart. Flustered by the attention, she said, "Thanks for coming to my rescue."

"I won't have any woman at SIA putting up with harassment."

"Thank you. You're a very nice man, Mr. Frasier."

He grinned, and she could swear a blush rose in his cheeks. "Thanks. Call me Ian, all right?"

Heat filled her center, and she eased into a smile to match his. "Okay."

"May I call you Synna?"

"Of course." After all, he had called her by her first name earlier!

Silence came over them, and then he broke in with, "You've worked here ten years, right? You moved up from entry-level secretary to head of records." He glanced around her modest digs. "I'm surprised you don't have an office of your own."

"They offered me an office, but I felt better able to communicate out here mingling with everyone else."

His glorious smile returned. "There aren't too many supervisors I know who would do that. Let me guess. Heidi is going into an office."

She nodded. "Mr. Monroe thinks it appears more professional, and she's jumping at the chance."

"I've already heard rumblings about the new arrangement."

Surprised, she asked, "From whom?"

"I directed human resources to let me know how this changeover works out. I like to keep my pulse on things, too. I think a supervisor who stays hidden in his or her office isn't always effective."

Impressed, she wished in a way she could stay here and enjoy the new directions he might take the agency. "What do you think? Should Heidi stay in a cubicle or have her own office?"

"I think she should keep a cubicle out here, but I'm willing to see how it works with her personality and how people respond to a more traditional supervisor."

She couldn't argue with his logic, and the fact that he cared what happened impressed her.

He spied a small framed photo she kept on a shelf near her desk and picked it up. "This is a beautiful picture. Is that you in the red velvet dress?"

"Yes. My sister Tanya is next to me with my mom and dad."

"You have a beautiful family."

"Thank you."

A pause came between them, just long enough for her to feel awkward.

"Can you spare a few minutes tomorrow morning?" he asked suddenly. "I need your opinion. That's why I originally stopped by in case you were still working."

Of course. He didn't stop by just to see me. No, that would be too ridiculous. "Certainly. How can I help?"

"I'll tell you then. Just stop by around nine o'clock if you've got time." His gaze narrowed, penetrating in a way that made her feel like she couldn't hide anything. "I'm sorry I didn't ask about this earlier. Do you have somewhere you need to be at that time? If you do, we could set up another time tomorrow."

She added considerate to his list of outstanding qualities. Good looks, brains, and thoughtfulness. A dangerous combination to the female heart.

"I have a meeting at eight o'clock, and I'm afraid it will run into nine o'clock." An idea came to mind. "What about earlier? I usually get in around seven o'clock."

He grinned. "That early, eh?"

She shrugged. "I like to beat traffic through the city."

"It's a date. I'm usually here around that time, too."

It's a date. Interesting way of putting it.

Intense and probing, his gaze seemed to ask for answers. Perhaps his proximity did it to her. She didn't feel stable with him near, as if she might say or do something unbelievably dumb. She loathed feeling like an out-of-control teen. She hadn't stuttered in months until this man appeared on the scene at SIA.

Instead of leaving, he came closer. When he towered over her, only a few inches away, her breath caught and her pulse did a wicked dance in her veins. "Do you need someone to walk you to your car?"

Taken by surprise, she spoke hastily. "Y-yes. I mean, no. Of course not. Why would I?"

"I'm concerned about your safety. I don't trust Tyler."

Pleasure settled inside her and she looked away, a little flustered. "Thank you for caring."

He reached out and tilted her chin up. The heat in his fingers sparked and danced over her skin. "You have a difficult time looking people in the eyes, don't you?"

His question took her completely off-guard. She couldn't deny the truth in what Ian said, even if she wanted. "Yes. I suppose people might think I was hiding something."

Ian released her chin, but he didn't step away. "Are you?"

Only that I think you're the most hunkiest guy I've ever seen, and I'd like to know what it feels like to be with you intimately? To know how your body would feel against me, deep inside me? Oh right. Like I can just let that information spill out.

"I never think much about it. I guess I learned to be that way when I was a child." She laughed softly. "Most people can't tell that I'm not looking them in the eyes. I stare at their lips or their chin and they don't know the difference. How can you tell?"

His voice lowered the timbre—husky, raw, and caressing. "I can read people very well, but I can't read you. I think it's just because you won't look *me* in the eye in particular."

Pain rushed across her psyche. God, she wanted know him better. To be truly understood by a man who appreciated her for what she was, for what she felt and thought. Sex might be an intimate connection of two bodies, but she craved the penetration of mind into mind, of feelings into feelings. True connection of souls she knew must be out there for her somewhere…if only she knew where to find it.

"But I have looked into your eyes." She let the floodgates open, eager to explain. "You just didn't see it. I'm stealthy that way. Besides, I pick up as much information about people intuitively. Body language is great, but sometimes even that can deceive."

Fascination colored his eyes deeper blue, the impact starting wildfire spirals deep in her loins. "What do you see in my eyes?"

In my wildest dreams, I see desire. A passion to make love to me.

"Intelligence and a strong determination to run SIA in the best way possible. Y-you want to make this new position work. You're compassionate, emphatic, and like you said, a keen observer."

He smiled a little. "Thank you. Is that all you see?"

This time she didn't do a hit-and-run when she gazed into his eyes. She really looked, sinking into his penetrating stare. Warmth swept into her as his eyes told her something she couldn't believe.

She thought she saw hunger increase, build like a storm ready to burst free. She couldn't say that to her boss. It would be suicide. "N-no…I can't see anything else."

A little ragged around the edges, his voice held urgency. "Then I guess I'll just have to show you."

Before she could blink, he plunged one hand into the hair at the back of her neck and drew her toward him until they touched. In reaction, her palms landed on his chest. His smooth sweater covered hard, tensile muscle that shifted under her tentative touch. Barely suppressed authority bunched and flexed, and she wanted to test his rigid muscle against all her inches.

Before anything else registered, he moved in and his mouth touched hers. Exquisite and gentle, he tasted and explored with a quick gesture that spelled fresh and new excitement. Pleasure spiked through her veins in wildfire explosions. His kiss came tentatively, as if he feared she might bolt.

She *should* run.

She *should* scram and never look back.

The head of SIA was kissing her.

Oh God.

How could she run when the man she'd fantasized about kissed the stuffing out of her and the pleasure almost brought her to her knees?

Synna's soft moan muffled against his lips as she responded mindlessly to the raging sexual inferno building inside. He might have moved away if she hadn't clutched his waist, her fingers encountering his belt as she searched for an anchor in the storm. Glorious sensations danced over her skin, popping like embers from a fire. As his mouth moved over hers with ravishing need, she felt dizzy and elated. Participating in the dance, she welcomed his kiss with wanton abandon and heady exhilaration. The kiss turned wild, consuming its own fuel, building like a fire overshadowing a tinder-dry forest. His mouth twisted this way, then that, tasting, moving her blood in a wild rush.

She wanted his tongue in her mouth, wanted him taking that last step to claim ownership.

Oh yes. This was the kiss she'd wanted, had waited for all her life.

Nothing had ever felt his good before.

Absolutely nothing.

He released her and stepped back, his chest rising with deep breaths. "God, I'm sorry." A stricken expression passed through his face, his eyes showing her everything. He looked horrified. "That was…" He shook his head. "Here I was telling you to watch out for Tyler, and I'm as bad as he is."

"Y-You've got to be kidding," she said impulsively, her pulse still rushing, body still aflame. "You're nothing like Tyler."

Remorse filled his face. "I'll be lucky if Level Ten doesn't fire me over this."

Alarmed, she took a step toward him. "Why? How could they know?" She looked around, wondering if anyone had seen them. All the cubicles appeared empty. "Do they have cameras in here spying on us?"

He didn't answer right away, and that satisfied her question.

"Oh no. They do," she said on a whisper.

"Damn it. Look, this was wrong." A pleading entered his eyes. "Pretend this didn't happen. I still need you to come to my office tomorrow morning. It's critical. But I promise I won't touch you."

I promise I won't touch you.

Those words sounded so damned depressing, she wanted to scream. What if she wanted him to touch her? That kiss had rocked her, set her blood on fire and melted her into a gooey mass of confusion.

"I'll be there," she said.

"I'll see you then. Have a good night," he said a little hoarsely. He left in a rush.

Her heart thumped with a combination of unexpected excitement, anticipation and utter dumbfounded surprise at what happened between them. As she watched him disappear around a corner, she didn't move. Shock rooted her to the spot.

No, what he'd done wasn't appropriate. What *she'd* done wasn't appropriate.

A twisted satisfaction made her grin. Ian Frasier, top dog at SIA, had swatted Tyler away from her like a pesky fly, then kissed her despite the fact cameras watched him.

He'd lost control, and she couldn't ever remember a man losing control like that with her.

On shaking legs, she sank down onto her chair and stared at the floor. This had been one hell of a day.

* * * * *

Ian strode across the SIA complex and headed for the Level Ten offices located in the subbasement. SIA was a twenty-four hour, seven days a week operation, but few people traversed the corridors this late at night, and even fewer people roamed the Level Ten area. Once in the elevator, he entered his security code, then placed his hand against the palm reader near the touchpad. The reader scanned and then sent the elevator down.

During the quick trip to the subbasement, he still had time to wonder how he could forget Synna for the rest of the evening.

He hadn't been on the job more than a few days before he'd been introduced to the administrative head of Division Two. With a name like Synna, a man could fantasize about what she looked like, and he did. He never listened to gossip, but he'd overheard two of the men in his office area making bets on whether Synna had lost her cherry yet. He'd walked up to the watercooler and had told them to stop speculating about her and get back to work.

A virgin at thirty-two? Not impossible, of course. The idea intrigued him. He'd never dated a virgin or slept with one, and the idea intrigued him the way it did most men, on a primal level.

She kept her glossy maple-colored hair cut shoulder-length, the waves loose and glorious. A side part meant her hair slid down a little on one side, and when she peeked out behind that curtain of hair, her gaze flirted with his libido.

Her eyes, a startling jade, had a slight almond tilt. While he could read most people with ease, he found her much harder to decipher. He'd seen more than one emotion in her gaze tonight. Fear, discomfort, curiosity, sadness and maybe…just maybe, a hint of interest in him as a man. With a strong jaw, she looked determined, yet her small nose and the elegant curve of her mouth spelled gentleness.

Her body…well, she'd worn a sweater dress one day that made everything male inside him want to touch and kiss and lick. Slim shoulders, full, lush breasts, a small waist and gently rounded hips completed the picture. She couldn't be more than five foot five and looked delicate.

Then there was that intriguing stutter that sometimes slipped into her sentences. He wondered if she'd always had it.

When he'd seen Tyler kissing Synna, Ian had wanted to run into the cubicle and jerk the asshole away. Even now, his anger over the incident hadn't diminished. He'd never felt this powerfully aroused, both mentally and physically, about a woman. It scared the crap out of him. She brought out primitive instincts he almost couldn't contain. Ian couldn't deny it, no matter how he tried to manipulate his feelings in a different direction.

He wanted to keep her safe and he wanted to fuck her.

Two very commanding, undeniable feelings.

Mortification burned deep inside him. If they said something to him about that kiss, he'd fess up. He admired Synna way beyond what even he'd understood until he'd realized she didn't look him directly in the eye. Her vulnerability had shaken his barriers loose.

"Fuck," he whispered.

When he talked to the members of Level Ten, he'd make them see they couldn't allow her to become involved with this project. Not only because she'd be working against a dangerous evil, but because his feelings for her went too far. He'd be damned if he'd let her get hurt, and with the subject of the investigation already stalking her, his concern escalated every day.

The elevator opened and he proceeded down the hall. When he reached the door to the conference room, he again used a palm reader. The metal pocket door slid into the wall and he stepped inside.

All except one member of the team sat at the black oval table in the center of the room. Eleven individuals comprised Level Ten. One associate always attended the meetings by intercom. No one ever saw her, and while not all of the members liked the idea that paranormal research librarian Dorcas "Dorky" Shannigan never attended the assembly in the flesh, they all understood why. The reason remained a tight secret within Level Ten. No one outside of Level Ten knew she belonged to their top-level group, even though many within SIA talked to her every day.

Skullduggery within skullduggery. Used to keeping secrets, he still found the situation with Ms. Shannigan amusing. Like most others within SIA, he depended on Dorky for her vast knowledge of the natural and the supernatural. Ian wished there had been someone like her when his unit in the army faced similar threats.

As he stepped into the room, the pocket door closed with a secure hiss. His glance came to the sideboard of fruit and pastries, coffee, soda and water. Notepads and pens lay on the table. Tonight he ignored the food and intended to proceed right to business. The team of men and women kept these meetings straight to the point. He'd set a friendly tone for the weekly summits, and he wanted to keep it that way. He hoped his arguments tonight wouldn't change the mood.

Ian took the chair at the head of the table. "Welcome everyone. Tonight's emergency meeting will be short."

"You just want the pastries." Rebecca Darnley, a seventy-year-old member of the board, grinned at him across the table, then licked frosting off her fingers.

"How did you guess?" he asked.

Gentle laughter filled the room as everyone finished grabbing their food from the sideboard, then settled into their chairs.

Mason Hingle, a balding and slightly pinch-faced, world-class computer genius, said, "I hear you're wearing an interesting costume to the party Halloween night."

Okay, so they didn't want to start off too seriously, apparently. "I don't know if it's that interesting. It's the first costume I've worn since I was ten years old, so this is kind of new to me."

Larina Farrah, a woman of about forty, swept her long black hair out of her eyes. Her liquid voice flowed over the room. "The last head of SIA wore a court jester outfit."

"I picked a very boring and easy-to-recognize outfit. I'm wearing my old battle dress uniform," Ian said.

"Poop green or Ode de Desert?" Oliver Greenbush, a former Navy officer, liked to tease Ian good-naturedly about the army.

"Desert. It's the last BDUs I wore. By the way, you planning on wearing the bubble head outfit?"

Oliver grimaced at the old moniker for submariners. "No way. I left the navy behind ten years ago."

Ian chuckled. "Guess I'm still prying the military background out my system." He shrugged. "Of course, I could always wear that medieval costume someone suggested."

Dorky's mellow, sexy voice came over the intercom. "Oh, I think you should wear it rather than the uniform. Mess your hair up a little, grow a beard the next two days, and you *might* make a good Aragorn from *Lord of the Rings*."

"Right," Ian said with a sardonic grin.

"Well, you do sort of look like him," Dorky said. "Minus the dark hair, of course."

"Women are always drooling all over that character. You might as well take advantage of it," Oliver said with hint of disgust.

Rebecca leaned over the table, enthusiasm for the subject spilling over her wrinkled features and into her words. "Good heavens, that's an excellent idea. You could keep that converter sword with you and no one would be wiser. Not even the other agents."

"Good point," Ian said.

An electrical converter sword would be an excellent weapon in case things went to shit at the party and Tyler did something stupid.

Like touching one hair on Synna's head.

Ian gulped. Damn it, he had it bad. Really bad.

Which costume would draw Synna's attention?

Ah shit. He really, really had to stop thinking of her like this. Every time he did, his cock ached.

He launched into serious business. "You all know why I called this meeting. I never thought I'd say this, but I thought I'd seen everything when I was in Alpha Unit. We dealt with plenty of creepy stuff, but what we're facing on Halloween this year is extremely dangerous. At our last meeting, you all proposed we get Synna MacDell involved because the subject has a crush on her. I'm here to tell you that we shouldn't."

Everyone in the room, even those munching on food, paused at his words.

"What exactly is your objection?" Darrell MacGraw asked from across the room.

"My objection is the same as it was at the last meeting. She's not a trained agent, and the subject alone is enough to freak out most anyone."

A few seconds later debate erupted, pros and cons tossed across the room.

He scribbled notes and waited for the dust to settle before putting forth his argument one more time. "Synna is leaving the SIA in a couple of weeks. We can't put her in danger."

"Every member of SIA is in jeopardy at any time from outside forces," Larina said. "Plus, she hasn't left the agency yet. She shouldn't be excluded from duty until she leaves."

"If she says no, you think I should order her to take on this assignment?" Ian asked.

One by one, every head nodded, and Dorky's soft voice chimed in at the end. "Yes."

Disappointment made him frown, but he couldn't say he was surprised by their stance. "I do this under protest, but I will insist that one thing *must* happen. She isn't going anywhere or seeing anyone without me keeping tabs on her. I'm sticking to her like spandex."

They agreed, and once the meeting ended, the social chatter lasted a few more minutes. After everyone left the room, he recalled that no one had called him the carpet. No one had given him a dirty look over a stolen kiss.

Then he realized Dorky left her intercom open. "Dorky?"

"Yes, Mr. Frasier."

"You think the Aragorn costume, eh?"

Her seductive laugh filtered over the air. "Oh, most definitely. She'll like it."

"Who?"

Her smooth voice continued. "Why, Synna, of course."

Shit. She must have seen the kiss. "I know you have access to the cameras in her area. I know you have access to *all* the security cameras. Did you happen to see—?"

"I saw the kiss. Don't worry. I cleaned up the tape. Wasn't that a little dangerous kissing her? I mean, Tyler kissed her and then you kissed Synna. Weren't you worried about transference? If she's tainted by Tyler's kiss, couldn't you be tainted by mouth-to-mouth contact with her? Did you—"

"No tongue." He laughed.

"Uh-huh. That's no guarantee."

"It's a pretty good one." *Sure. You just couldn't keep from kissing her, despite the danger.*

He heard material shifting, then a chair squeaking. "Are you planning on ratting me out to Level Ten?"

"Your secret is safe with me. Humans can and should fall in love in the workplace. The head can't always rule the heart."

Humans? The way she said that word made him wonder what she meant.

Before he could ask, she said, "I'm back to work now. Talk with you tomorrow."

The intercom disconnected and left him with traitorous thoughts of Synna and her intoxicating taste remaining on his lips.

Ian didn't want the raging sexual energy he'd felt between them to disappear from his life. Yet, he couldn't ask her to have a relationship with him while still an employee of the SIA. Being around her, protecting her from Tyler, would take all his energy and concentration. If he wanted to develop his connection with her, he would need to do it without jeopardizing his career or her good name.

* * * * *

Heat seared Ian as he wrestled with a dream that wouldn't let go.

Synna wore nothing but a lustful gleam in her eye. She stood by his bed, skin gleaming golden under firelight as it danced in the grate. His eyes adjusted to the dimness as he absorbed her beauty. She wandered toward the bed where he lay spread-eagle and awaited her first touch. His cock ached with need, dying to find the tightness between her legs. He could smell her musky arousal, could almost taste it on his tongue. God, how he'd like to spread her long legs and lick her clit. He knew her taste would be creamy and delicious, a sweet heaven he must experience. He licked his lips and groaned. Nothing would please him more.

Heat rose from the fireplace and the red glow shimmered behind her as she stepped to the side of the bed, then climbed on to straddle him. As she nestled her warm, wet pussy against the side of his cock, Ian gasped. Searing sensations tingled through his body, yearning, building as she slid her pussy against him and leaned forward. Her naked breasts pressed against his chest. Hard nipples brushed over his pecs, and he moaned as he reached up to cup the sides of her breasts. Her beguiling smile tortured him as much as the press of her lithe body. She leaned forward and pressed a sizzling kiss to his mouth, and he responded instantly, wanting her taste. Minty and fresh, her mouth brushed over his again and again. He shivered, unable to hide his reaction. He lifted his hips, wanting to slide his heat high and tight into her depths.

"Please, baby," he murmured against her mouth. "Take me. I've got to have you."

She laughed, the sound gentle as her hands drifting up to cup his face. As his touch found her hips, she lifted and slid down over his cock until her heat encompassed his rock-hard erection.

He groaned and writhed beneath her, shifting his hips upward and starting a pumping motion. Liquid heat moved up and down upon him, tight and silky. His motion quickened as she rode him. He heard her soft moans, the little whimpers in her throat that signaled her enjoyment and it set him off.

He wanted her in this moment and forever.

Ian broke out of the dream with a start. In the dim light from a night light in the bathroom, he half expected to see Synna walking toward him. His cock stood hard and angry. Fuck it. He needed release.

His hand wrapped around his cock, and he hissed in a breath. Oh yeah. That was better. Not as hot and silky as Synna's depths would feel when he got into her. He closed his eyes and imagined the scenario in his dream in full detail. With slow, steady strokes, he satisfied his need. He used the pre-cum from the tip of his cock to moisten his glide. He fisted his grip tighter around the rigid flesh.

She'd be so hot, so incredible, so tight. Her breasts would feel soft and round against his chest, her nipples aroused and begging for his touch. As her hips moved, she'd lowered her breasts over his mouth. He tongued them, first one and then the other. She would moan as he suckled her nipples without mercy.

From dream to the fantasy, he fell straight into another world. His cock grew harder by the second, his fist moving up and down until the pleasure tightening his loins demanded fulfillment. He moaned continuously until he roared out a bone-melting climax. His cock jerked as long streams of cum spurted from him. Ian panted through his mouth as his heartbeat slowed from a frantic pace.

"Shit, Frasier, you haven't done that in a long time."

At least, not until he met Synna MacDell. Now he swore he could jack off every night and it wouldn't eliminate the longing that invaded his body and his mind.

Chapter Three

Synna arrived at the parking garage by six-thirty the next morning and sat in her car for another five minutes trying to resurrect her nerve. Since her encounter last night with Ian, self-conscious obsessions had assaulted her. At one time, lack of confidence held her back from life, but she'd conquered that long ago. Old insecurities threatened to roar back to life.

Ian's kiss had sent her world into a tailspin. She hadn't slept well last night. She replayed the kiss inside her head to the point of nauseating tedium.

"You are insane," she whispered.

She should be more concerned about this strange meeting with Ian and with what happened with Tyler yesterday. She took several deep, steadying breaths to clear her head.

As she looked around the parking structure, she felt a creepy sense that someone watched her. Hairs all over her body prickled with awareness. Danger seemed to lurk in every innocent corner. Like a phobic, she let the panic take her to wild places in her mind to horrific scenarios.

"Snap out of it," she said aloud. "This isn't like you."

She took another deep breath to steady overactive nerves and left her car for Division Two. She stopped by her cubicle to dump off her trench coat and her small black organizer handbag. Thank God, no one else seemed insane enough arrive at work in her section this early. She quickened her pace and headed for the elevator.

Anxiety made her hesitate as she headed for the elevator. She'd taken an extra fifteen minutes this morning standing in her walk-in closet trying to decide what to wear. Pants? A suit? She'd settled on a comfortable ensemble she didn't have the guts to wear until this morning. The outfit included a form-fitting ruby red top with a scoop neck, three-quarter sleeves, and a calf-length black skirt that arrowed close to her body. Stretchy material slicked along her curves in a way that said sexy without screaming slut. Black hose and modest-heeled black pumps completed the picture. She'd taken time with her makeup and hair, leaving the flowing waves streaming over her shoulders. A set of orb-shaped plain onyx earrings and matching necklace almost completed the picture. She also wore her signature rings, a large amethyst on her right hand and a swirling pinky ring of white, pink, and yellow gold on her left hand.

She felt like a million and a half bucks, but as she stepped into the elevator she wondered what possessed her. Why had she gone to so much more effort than before? Sure, she dressed professionally for work every day, but today she'd dressed like she'd planned a date with Ian.

Heat flushed her face as she pushed the button for his floor. *Oh boy.* She'd done it. She wanted to please a man, and she hadn't done that in so long she couldn't recall the last time.

You've lost your mind, Synna.

Ian Frasier found her attractive or he wouldn't have kissed her, but he also seemed to truly like women on the whole. One kiss didn't mean he wanted her to have his babies.

Sexual stirrings coiled tightly in her stomach at the thought. The idea of having a man's baby had never stirred sexual feelings inside her before, until now.

Oh God. I have it bad.

All her senses heightened, working toward a fiery meltdown of anticipation.

Aroused.

Dying for his kiss.

When the elevator door dinged, she started. Several people tried piling on the elevator before she could exit, and two of the men in the group gave her a blatant once-over. Now she knew her clothes could attract a man's attention. What would it do to Ian? She pushed passed the people crowding into the elevator and into the hallway.

As she hurried toward his office, she wondered why he couldn't have asked her opinion when he came to her cubicle last night? What could be so important?

She arrived at the large mahogany double doors on the first floor that held his offices. As she entered, she noted the reception desk where his secretary normally sat was empty. The door to his office stood open, and she heard the faint tones of smooth jazz. She started to call out when he walked through the door and they collided.

Synna would have bounced off him, but he caught her upper arms in a gentle grip. Plastered chest to thigh against Ian, she felt the heat and hardness in his big frame. Her breath caught in her throat, pleasure rousing inside her at his closeness.

Flustered, she said, "Oh, I'm s-sorry."

"No problem." His smile, a little cocky and teasing, curved his gorgeous mouth. "I was about to start a pot of coffee. Would you like some?"

She shook her head. "None for me, thanks. I've had too much already."

"Maybe I'll skip it for now, too. You're early."

She couldn't help smiling. "Story of my life. I'm chronically early."

"Sounds like a great habit to me."

His hands slid up to her shoulders, and the hot imprint of his touch through her top made her feel vulnerable. His eyes burned into hers, and for a moment, her pulse fluttered and she couldn't get her breath.

He hadn't shaved, and the shadow along his jawline, along with his hair hanging loose around his shoulders, gave him an untamed edge that screamed sexy. His subtle scent made all her desires arise and take notice. He smelled so delicious. His gaze did an almost imperceptible sweep down to her breasts, and yet the intensity of his attention felt like a brand. Male appreciation flashed through the ocean depths in his eyes, then flickered out.

He let her go, and she didn't know whether to rejoice or wish he still touched her. "How is your knee?"

"It's fine. There isn't much of a bruise."

She lifted the hemline of her skirt to show him. The darker bruise showed through the sheer black hose. Heat sluiced through her as his attention traveled down her body to reach her knee instead of skipping right to the injured area.

Then his interest changed as his lips tightened. "That's not a little bruise."

She shrugged. "It'll be fine in a few days."

He nodded, but he didn't look too pleased. "Please come in."

She wandered into his office after him, and tried not to ogle his ass like a lovesick teenager. This morning he wore a deep copper sweater that skimmed along his muscled torso enough to reveal serious development of biceps and forearms. Along his rib cage, the sweater hugged his torso down to his flat stomach. Black pants made his legs look even longer. She felt tiny against his undeniable brawn. He made her feel feminine down to her shoes.

His large office had no windows, but he'd left on a lamp near a loveseat at one end of the room, and another small green banker's lamp glowed on his desk. Recessed lighting in the ceiling also warmed the room. He'd changed a few things from the last administrator to hold this post. He'd furnished the area with light wood furniture, Swedish influence and Mission design in a combination eclectic but exquisite. Though modern, the décor held warmth she wouldn't have expected.

"Your office is beautiful," she said.

He settled onto the edge of his desk. "Thank you. I would have kept Dr. Franchett's furniture but it was splintering and falling apart."

She nodded and smiled. "It *was* looking a little ratty."

Her gaze snagged on an eight-by-ten photograph nestled on the bookshelves behind his desk. A beautiful blonde woman with long, curly hair stood next to him in the photograph. They looked perfect together.

A strange sinking sensation entered her stomach. "What a striking picture."

He turned and looked. "That's my favorite photograph."

"I didn't know you were married."

"I'm not." He turned and retrieved the photo, then held it out to her.

Puzzled, she took the pewter-scroll frame and examined the photo. Obviously, the background was in a studio setting. He wore a black suit and she wore a lime green jacquard dress. Synna took a closer look and thought she saw a resemblance in the woman to Ian across the eyes and jawline.

"Is she your sister?"

Another handsome smile carved his gorgeous mouth. "That's Patti, my mother."

Her mouth popped open in surprise and embarrassment. She gave a nervous laugh. "S-she looks so young."

He crossed his arms, his gaze indulgent and warm. "She had me when she was sixteen. She's an incredible self-made woman. Her parents disowned her when she got pregnant with me."

Sympathy pinched her heart. "What did she do then?"

"She asked my Aunt Lillie if she could live with her, and Aunt Lillie agreed wholeheartedly. Mom finished high school, got a job, went to community college, and became an interior designer."

She handed him the photograph and he returned it to the bookshelf. Admiration made her say, "That's fabulous. She never married?"

"As a matter of fact, she's engaged. The wedding is Christmas Eve."

"You'll have a stepfather for the first time."

He stared at the photograph for an intense moment. "I'm looking forward to it. My father died five years ago."

When he returned to the edge of the desk, she impetuously reached out and touched his shoulder. "I'm so sorry about your loss."

Seated on the side of his desk, he looked at ease, nothing like a stereotypical head of a major intelligence agency with branches in several different countries. What kind of man did it take to run such a complex system and survive the politics and the stress? Looking at his face now, she saw lines of character between his brows and around his eyes, but he didn't look any older than his thirty-six years.

"Thank you. He was an SIA agent and was killed on assignment."

Astonished, she gasped. "Oh my God." She shifted gears, curiosity eating her up. "How long was he with SIA?"

"For ten years. Before that he was in the navy."

"What was his name? Maybe I knew him."

"Jonathan Frasier."

She nodded. "The name sounds familiar, but I don't recall meeting him."

He shrugged. "Dad spent most of his time in the field. You may not have run into him."

She processed this information before speaking again. "Did you know him since you were a child?"

"Off and on when he came onto dry land. He was a good man. Mom and Dad realized they were both too young to marry when they first met."

Denise A. Agnew

"And they never wanted to reunite when they were older?"

In an uncharacteristic gesture of uncertainty, he stuffed his hands in his pants pockets. "Dad wasn't the marrying type. He liked his risky careers far more than he did settling down with one woman."

"Did you join the SIA because of him?" The moment she said the words his expression went taut, and she at once regretted her hasty question. "I'm sorry. It's none of my business."

She sensed unease inside him, and she wondered if he wished he hadn't told her personal information. "No, it's all right. I was in the army since I was eighteen, and during that time, I saw almost all the adventure I needed."

"Yet you're employed by one of the most adventurous organizations on earth." She grinned, taking a chance and teasing him.

To her relief, he returned the smile. "During my army career I worked for a unique organization of soldiers specifically qualified to investigate and fight the unusual."

She'd heard of them, and her admiration for him went up another notch. "Alpha Unit?"

He nodded and crossed his arms. "That's the one. I headed up a team within the unit."

His concentrated gaze traveled over her features, assessing her in that all-encompassing way that made her nipples tighten and her lower belly pool with heat. Synna stood too close to his disturbing masculinity, and she took a few steps away until she could sit on the loveseat.

"It sounds like you and your mother make a wonderful family." Hurt centered her heart as she thought about her own fractured family. "That's a precious thing to have."

"I'm glad she's in love and happy."

Love.

His velvety tone, so deep and mellow, sent warm trickles of awareness over her body. She couldn't deny she felt better now she knew about his single status. Part of that realization ticked her off. So what if he was single? One impetuous kiss and she thought she owned him?

Ian seemed to break out of his reverie. "I'm sorry. I'm keeping you too long."

"It's all right." The longer she talked to him, the more she wanted to stay. "What can I help you with?"

He grabbed a straight-backed chair, turned it around and straddled it. He leaned his arms on the chair back. "What I need to ask you is more than a big favor. And after what I saw happen with Tyler last night, I can see that I was right to fight against including you in this project. Hell, with what I did, I wouldn't blame you if you refused."

Instinctively, she stiffened at his statement. Why would he fight against including her unless he didn't think she could do the assignment?

He continued. "There's a mission I need you to tackle. I want you to hear me out before you object to what I want you to do."

Her nerves started to rebel, the tension tight. "I'm listening."

Ian pushed one hand through the thick length of his hair. Light glinted off the strands and reddish highlights gleamed. *God, did he have any idea how overwhelmingly gorgeous he was?*

Grim-faced, he abandoned the chair and moved to sit on the loveseat near her. She inhaled a little sharply, startled by his sudden change in venue. She couldn't ignore his edge, the ferocity in his depthless gaze. He had mentioned last night she didn't look him in the eye, but now she couldn't seem to stop staring straight into those mesmerizing windows to his soul.

"I argued against the entire plan from the moment Level Ten suggested it," he said.

By now, his hesitation to tell her ate a hole in her patience, but she tempered her statement. "Sounds intense."

"It's dodgy."

A prickling feeling, a caution, made her lean against the back of the loveseat.

"I need you to go with Tyler to the Halloween party," he said.

Chapter Four

ಬಿ

Synna's eyes widened, surprise keeping her silent for fifteen seconds before she spoke. "What?"

"I know it goes against what happened with him yesterday. I argued against this entire setup with Level Ten, but they filibustered and demanded that you be a part of this project."

Baffled by the turn in events, she glared at him. "But you're the Chief Executive Officer and Director."

"If there's a serious situation they feel needs immediate action, they can overrule my decisions. That way the head of SIA can't abuse his or her power."

"I see," she said softly.

His gaze turned intent, filled with cynical doubt. She fidgeted with her necklace, rubbing the smooth surface. "Why would Level Ten be concerned about me going out with Tyler?"

Ian's eyes held contrition. "Because he's not what he appears to be."

"A spy?"

"I wish that was all. No, this is much worse."

Chills coasted over her body, and she stood and paced the room. "A traitor?"

"Not exactly."

Frustrated, she stalked toward him. "Ian, can we stop playing charades and just get to the bottom of this?"

"Let me start at the beginning. Tyler began work at SIA less than six months ago. He went through psychological and physical screening like everyone else. Unfortunately, his condition isn't currently detectable until it's too late."

"Is he ill?"

"No. He's possessed."

She couldn't have heard him right. She stopped fumbling with the necklace. "What? You mean like in *The Exorcist*? Spinning heads and everything?"

"No. He's *the* demon. A weredemon."

Now she'd heard it all. Despite knowing the SIA dealt with the paranormal on a regular basis, the supernatural hadn't touched her much in thirty-two years.

One of his eyebrows tilted upward in question. "You look stunned."

"It's not every day the head of SIA tells me I've got to date a weredemon. Whatever that is."

A quick smile passed over his lips. "A weredemon is capable of transforming into a human when it wants."

She clutched the back of the chair he'd sat on a few moments ago. Her heart thumped a little harder, and her pulse drummed faster. Alarm started a slow encroachment, threatening to unravel her, one nerve at a time.

God, if this wasn't a crazy turn of events. She didn't know if she could say yes to the assignment, even if the most intriguing man she'd met had just asked her to do it.

She reached for her necklace again and clutched it. "You're not going to tell me there's a real hell and the SIA has found it?"

He chuckled softly. "The SIA doesn't need to find it. Hell is a state of mind, not a place. The weredemons are from the Shadow Realm, a purgatory where lost souls wander and mingle with a few other unsavory beings."

When she digested the mind-boggling information, she asked, "Tell me this is a joke my coworkers set up to freak me out in my last few weeks at SIA."

"Afraid not. I know this comes as a shock. When I worked with Alpha Unit, we fought these forces more than once. Over the years the SIA and other government agencies have discovered these creatures exist."

"Creatures," she murmured with a dry throat. "So there are other things besides demons to worry about. Ghosts? Vampires? Werewolves?"

He stood and crossed the short space between them to look down at her, amusement dancing in his eyes. "All three. Most ghosts, vampires or werewolves aren't a danger to humans. They have good and bad among them."

"Where is this Shadow Realm, by the way?"

His lips tightened. "Another dimension. It's complicated, but it has to do with leaks in the wormholes between one dimension and another. That's why people can sometimes see ghosts."

"So werewolves and vampires are from this other dimension."

"No. They are here on earth with us and have been for many hundreds of years. Weredemons and quite a few other creatures belong to the Shadow Realm only."

She groaned. "It's a good thing most people don't know about this paranormal stuff. They'd be scared out of their wits."

"You can say that again."

She let out a short laugh. "It sounds absurd. I accepted that a long time ago that the SIA was out there fighting terrorists and the paranormal, but I never thought I'd be a part of the fight face-to-face."

"If you doubt me, you can call Dorky Shannigan. She'll confirm it."

"No. No, I believe you."

She rubbed her palms over her arms. Excitement mixed with dread, and she didn't know what to do. "Why do I need to go with Tyler—I mean, the weredemon—to this party? Fresh meat?"

A muscle in his jaw worked. "God no. I'll do everything in my power to keep you safe."

Passion in his eyes trapped Synna, kept her from speaking. He moved closer and soon barely six inches separated them. Now her heartbeat sped up from his potent nearness and not from trepidation of the unknown. How could a man inspire heady sexual awareness and pure safety at the same time? He made her feel sheltered and yet on the cusp, her body so tuned into his she wanted to reach out and touch him. Her loins melted, her nipples tightened.

"I don't understand why you just can't use some SIA trick to get this weredemon. You can't just go to Tyler's house, surround him SWAT style and be done with it?" she asked.

"I wish it was that simple."

"Why isn't it?"

"Weredemons have very good extrasensory perception. They can sense when people are lying. There are people, like me, with very controlled minds. We can't be brainwashed. Because we can't be brainwashed, a weredemon can't influence us or take thoughts from our minds."

A realization dawned. "Oh my God. That's why you're using me. Because I have a strong mind and I'm intuitive like the weredemon. Therefore, he can't read my mind or detect what I might do. He must still think I'm completely incapable of deceiving him, when it really is that he can't brainwash me."

"Correct."

"So if the team went in to take him out at his home, he'd get wind of it through one of the team member's mind. He'd be long gone before the mission to capture him could be pulled off. Am I right?"

Ian grinned. "You're absolutely right. It's freakin' incredible how right you are." Serious and hard, his gaze found hers. "It's the only reason why I want you on this assignment. He can't read your mind at all and it drives him nuts. He wants to know you better. He's also sexually attracted to you."

"Ewww. I already know that."

"Try not to let him gross out you out, or he'll realize it because of your body language."

She almost cringed. "This is going to take some work. I didn't like him much before I knew what he really was, but now...yuck."

He chuckled, his gaze dancing with hers in total amusement. "That's very descriptive, you know? A damned girly thing to say, but it says it all."

"Of course it's girly." Protest entered her voice. "I'm a woman."

Ian's gaze snapped up to hers. He inhaled, the motion moving his big chest and drawing her attention. "Yeah, I know."

The way he emphasized the words echoed in her head.

She couldn't keep uncertainty out of her voice. "I-I'm not a trained agent."

"I know. That isn't what made me want to keep you out of this situation."

"What is it?"

"When I kissed you yesterday that was inexcusable, but I'm going to just break down right now and tell you why I kissed you. If it means my ass is grass and Level Ten finds out and decides to kick my butt out onto the concrete, so be it. I've never been one to pull punches, and I think that's one of the reasons why they hired me." He took a deep breath. "Ever since the first moment I saw you, I felt something hot between us. I thought at first it might be my imagination, but I realized that whenever we met I felt this connection." He cracked a weary smile. "If the way I feel in any way makes you uncomfortable, please tell me right now."

Her jaw dropped again, and this time she didn't think she'd recover. What could she say to an unexpected confession like that?

When she didn't speak, his mouth twisted a little. "Damn, if I screw this up any more than—"

"No," she said a little sharply. Again, she reached out and touched his arm. The tight strength in his biceps sent excitement whirling through her belly. "You haven't. I'm just surprised. I thought maybe there was a little something between us, but I also wondered if it could be my imagination." A horrifying thought slipped through. "Did Level Ten see you kiss me?"

He gave her a warm smile. "Apparently Dorky did but she ignored it. She let me know in an understated way that she didn't plan on telling any of the others. I have a feeling the kiss is going to disappear from the visual record."

Wide-eyed, she asked, "She can do that?"

"You'd be amazed at what she can do."

She heard admiration in his voice for the mysterious librarian. "She's a special woman."

He leaned in a little closer, his voice husky. "You're more than special. You're damned near intoxicating." His gaze danced up and down her body. "Did you wear that top and skirt to drive me nuts?"

His bluntness no longer served to astonish her, and she plunged right into her own honesty. "I think maybe I did."

"You're not sure?"

Feeling a little mischievous, she winked. "Okay, I'm sure. I did wear them for you."

"Well, you've succeed in catching my interest. I've been fighting a hard-on from the moment you ran into me this morning."

She blushed violently. "Ian."

Answering moisture dampened the folds between her legs, and she almost moaned at the torturing arousal growing moment by moment. She felt so out of control, she didn't know if she could stand the spiraling need.

He reached out and cupped her waist, drawing her into him until her body molded lightly against his sinewy frame. His long, thick cock pressed against her stomach. "I swore I wouldn't touch you, but damn it—"

Synna placed her index finger over his lips. "It makes me feel...I don't know...good to think you can't keep your hands off me."

Oops, did I just say that?

"I was hoping it would make you feel more than good."

She let her hands slide upward over his chest, and when her fingers passed over his hard nipples, he gasped a little. Her inhibitions started to crack. His body shuddered, a little shiver that signaled she affected him down deep where it mattered. Female satisfaction, primitive and undeniable, settled inside her.

"I suppose we should be talking about the mission," she said, feeling breathless.

Ian blinked, then shook his head. "Yeah. We should be." He released her and moved back a step. "I'm trying to think where to start with this crazy story."

"Continue where you left off. Weredemons are from the Shadow Realm and you object to me taking on this mission. Why?"

Aggravation took over the concern in his eyes. "Because a weredemon is a hell of a lot more difficult to deal with than a human adversary."

"How did the SIA know Tyler is a weredemon in the first place?"

He walked around to his desk. "Weredemons are detected when a blood test is performed. Their chemical makeup doesn't come out quite like a human's. Tyler had blood taken three weeks ago during the annual office blood drive. Because the SIA knows these supernatural beings exist, the labs do a special screening whenever blood is taken for any reason. Once you've had sex with a weredemon, your chemistry is permanently changed."

A little puzzled, she clasped the back of the chair near the couch. "Wait a minute, are you saying Tyler could have just had sex with a weredemon and his chemistry would be changed? What if he's not a weredemon at all?"

He scrubbed a hand over his stubble-rough jaw. "There is a difference in chemical structure from someone who has sex with the weredemon and an actual weredemon. A few people in the agency who can detect otherworldly beings felt someone or something penetrate the agency. They just didn't know who or where. The blood drive was a lucky draw for us. We would have had to do mandatory blood testing to detect where the creature was."

She pressed her fingers to her temples. "This is amazing and so bizarre." Other questions popped to mind. "What exactly do these weredemons want? Why do they come here? To make general mayhem?"

He grabbed a hand strengthener made of foam off his desk and squeezed it repetitively. Watching his strong hand flex made the steady tingle in her stomach expand.

"If they were just mischievous," he said, "it wouldn't matter so much. They're highly intelligent and crafty in a way you can't imagine."

"Oh, I don't know. I can imagine a whole lot. Tell me more about the weredemons."

She half-dreaded knowing while another part of her must know. How could she survive the mission otherwise?

He seemed unsatisfied, itching to question her. "Hundreds of years ago they realized if they mated with humans, they could then change into human form at will. A half-human, half-demon combo."

Synna's active imagination did a flinch at the idea. No, it sounded plausible. Nauseating but real. Confusion added to the mix. "Wait a minute. A demon from the Shadow Realm comes into our realm and mates with a human. That's what makes a weredemon?"

"Yes, but there are no pure demons left any more in the Shadow Realm. All of them have mixed with human blood. They've been half-breeds for centuries."

"So when they kiss a human, they change the human's chemical makeup and therefore make it possible for them to breed again with a human?"

He frowned. "You got it."

"Wouldn't their offspring be even more diluted? More human if they kept breeding over and over with humans?"

"We're not sure about that yet. Our labs are still trying to figure it out. If they mate with a human they also obtain more powers. They can sometimes procreate, sometimes not. If they do procreate, the half-demon, half-human can be pretty powerful on his own," he said.

"What kind of powers?"

"Ability to influence human behavior in the extreme."

Dread snaked across her skin with a cold shiver. "T-That's horrible. How long have they been trying to breed with humans?"

"Like I said, hundreds of years. Pretty much forever."

"Gee, that's comforting." Disturbed, she wrestled with emotions she couldn't define. Fear? Uncertainty? "You sound so matter-of-fact, so unaffected. Just an hour ago—two hours now—I stood in front of my mirror and changed clothes for the third time. That was the most important thing in my life. Now, weredemons take precedence."

A grin tilted his handsome mouth. "It took you three changes before you decided on that outfit?"

A blush stole over her face. "Yes." She didn't want to dwell on what she'd admitted. "What do you want me to do? Approach Tyler and ask for a date?"

"You'll approach him today and say you've changed your mind. Obviously, he intends to mate with you."

Sickened by the idea, she made a little face. "How exactly do I pretend to like him back without...without him thinking he really can m-mate with me?"

His glower made little lines form on his forehead. "That's part of the reason why I was angry when I saw him kiss you. Even kissing a weredemon can create havoc with your system. You need to go to medical and tell them you've been compromised by a weredemon. They'll do a series of tests."

Fear started a slow, inevitable slide into her, along with a little anger. "Are you telling me I might already be—? That...that creep may have changed my chemical composition already?"

"Take it easy. He probably didn't kiss you long enough to make a huge difference. It has to be prolonged physical contact, and he has to want to change you. One of the benefits for the weredemon is once they make love with a human and turn that person's chemistry, the victim is joined with that weredemon for life."

"Oh God."

"Now you understand why I didn't want you doing this?" She looked into his clear eyes. Fire reigned in them. "He's probably genuinely interested in you as a mate and wants to make love with you." He winked. "I can't blame him for that."

A new desire raged inside her, this one melting with a need to take what she wanted. Without a doubt, she wanted Ian. Here and now.

He must have seen her panic or maybe her desire, for he reached out and cupped her face in both of his big hands. His touch was a mix of fierce tenderness and assurance. "Oh shit." His words came out as a groan. "This is insane. I can't let you do this. I'll go against Level Ten—"

"N-no." She reached up and clasped his forearms. "I'll go up to him today and say I've changed my mind and want to go with him to the party."

His thumbs caressed her cheeks. The sensual wave filling her center frightened her deep inside where she didn't often examine or dwell, where her most heinous fears lurked in wait to ambush when least expected.

Desire passed through his gaze, unvarnished and raw. Her palms slid up his forearms to clasp his wrists. Need flickered like a flame, scorching her with cravings too severe to contain.

Recklessly, Synna reached up and touched his jaw, a quick feel of prickly stubble against her fingers. "This is a new look for you."

He drew in a little breath, as if her touch startled him or turned him on. "It's a part of my costume for the party."

Intrigued, she smiled. "What are you going to be?"

One of his eyebrows quirked in amusement and his deep voice took on a husky timbre. "You'll have to wait and see."

"The anticipation is going to kill me."

"You can't wait until Halloween night?"

"I'd rather not."

A soft laugh rumbled up from deep in his chest, and the male sound brushed already aroused senses into full flower. He called to her heart as well as her baser needs, and because it frightened her a little at how easily he seduced her, Synna drew back.

She walked away until she stood less than a few feet from a painting on a wall. Shades of pink adorned a Victorian woman with a parasol. It should have looked too feminine in this office, but the fact Ian had it here showed Synna that he felt secure in his masculinity. Other more manly paintings graced the room. Boats, foxhunts and rugged landscapes.

Even the calm repose in the Victorian woman's face couldn't distract her from what might happen Friday night at the party.

"I've got to do this. If you use someone else to do this assignment, he'll get suspicious. He's not a dumb man...demon."

His footsteps, muffled by the thick carpet, sounded behind her.

When he stood behind her, so close they almost touched, he said, "Are you absolutely positive?"

"Yes."

He heaved a sigh, then his breath touched her neck. "Don't let him get this close." He brushed her hair aside, his hot breath touching her left ear. "Don't let him touch you like this."

Sweet, melting pleasure pooled in her loins. "Ian."

Longing trembled inside Synna, torturing her into leaning back the bit required to touch Ian, her back to his chest, her buttocks against his thighs. With this man, there seemed to be no holding back.

His hands came down on her shoulders. Yet his stroke held a weight, a meaningfulness she experienced deeply. Nerves dissolved, replaced by drugging sensuality. She fought for a semblance of control.

"How can I keep him from touching me if he's my date?" Her words sounded rusty and afraid.

Again, his breath tickled her left ear, his voice softer and deeper. "I won't let you out of my sight. Several other agents will watch out for you. You'll lead him out to the park area outside the SIA. We'll nab him when he makes his move to mate with you."

Anxiety tried to intrude, but she shoved it ruthlessly aside. "I never thought dating could be hazardous to my health."

"You know how I feel about this. Do you trust me?"

Synna didn't have to think about it. "Of course."

"I have a theory on how to defeat the weredemon, but I need to check it out with Dorky first." He kissed her ear, as lightly and exquisitely as a feather.

"What's the theory?"

He smoothed his hands over her shoulders down to her upper arms. Still nestled against him, she almost purred at the soul-deep pleasure. "I don't know if I should tell you until I confirm if it's true. I don't want you to feel pressured or think I'm trying to take advantage of you."

She turned slowly toward him, his hands dropped to his sides. "I trust you, Ian."

"Good. There's a ritual we can perform before the Halloween party that can assure the weredemon can't harm you, even if he manages to kiss you again."

She shrugged. "How hard can it be? What do we have to do?"

Ian sighed, his eyes now darkened by misgiving. "It involves sexual activity."

She almost gulped. "S-sexual activity."

"If that is what it takes."

Surprised, she didn't say anything at first. When she found her voice, she managed a cheeky question even though she already knew the answer. "With whom?"

He crossed his arms, his gaze intent and not the least amused. "With me, of course."

Chapter Five

ॐ

Synna's mouth popped open as she absorbed his shocking proposal. Doubt crept around her heart, confusion not far behind. Could he be trying to deceive her? Irritation wedged around the haze of sensual pleasure she'd found with him moments ago.

"What if I don't want to have sex with you?" she asked.

He towered over her, his strength and charisma cranking her libido back into high gear. "Synna, I'm not playing games here. I'm laying it on the line. I've wanted you more than any woman I've ever known from the first time I saw you." He lowered his voice, the nuance a husky whisper imbued with delicious undertones. "Our kiss should tell you how attracted I am to you, but if you need another demonstration—"

She put her hand on his chest in reaction. Any more kisses and she'd combust on the spot. "No. That's all right. I believe you."

Silence reigned while he measured her with a probing look. "I know it sounds bogus as hell. That's why we should confirm it with Dorky. I'll telephone her right now and when she finds out if the ritual is something that could help us, she'll telephone you directly so you know it's legit."

Feeling a bit overwhelmed, she started for the door. "This is almost too much, Ian."

She barely reached the door when he caught her by the shoulder and gently swung her around. She backed up against the door in defense, suspicion rising where once she'd felt trust.

Blue eyes stared into hers, daring her to say that she didn't want anything to do with him. "No matter what you believe, Synna, know this. Tyler is a dangerous creature and it scares me to think you could be hurt. In your dealings with him today, make sure you don't let him get you alone. Okay?"

His index finger drew a caressing line down her cheek. With deliberate slowness, he edged nearer. Blazing with heat, the sexual intent in those mysterious eyes was unmistakable. His lips captured hers and the pressure searched but didn't demand. She didn't think, she reacted to the feral heat glowing like embers deep inside the moist need of her pussy. A little whimper left her throat, and she slipped her arms around his neck and pressed her body to his. His arms drew her hard against him. His hard cock nudged her belly, insistent and unmistakable. Before they could deepen the kiss, she drew back with a gasp. He kept her tucked against him, a frown tightening his lips.

Nothing could hide his want or deny the way she felt. She felt itchy with desire, and tremendous need to learn more about him and take this relationship to a deeper level. Physical craving dominated, but she knew that was only temporary without understanding more about him as a person.

"I hope there isn't a camera in here," she said.

An appreciative grin flitted over his lips. "No."

"Good." She reached behind her and turned the lock on the door.

"Holy shit," he said softly.

"Exactly."

"I can't believe we're doing this."

"Neither can I. We barely know each other."

Hesitation lasted maybe two seconds, but the inferno grew between them, and she knew she must have one more taste in case she never had another chance.

Synna cupped his face this time, savoring the prickle of stubble against her fingers. She drew him down for another kiss. Caution faded as she swept her tongue over his lips, telling him what she wanted. With a twist of his lips, he plunged his tongue inside, stroking deep.

A muffled groan escaped her. Her stomach clenched and tingled as his tongue rubbed against hers, unrelenting and communicating what she longed to experience in a deeper, more sexual way. Her pussy moistened, slick and growing hotter by the second. An ache built in her core, tight and throbbing. Captured by sensation, she committed this moment to memory.

Aggressive stabs of his tongue searched out every hidden erogenous zone. Big, hot hands tested her skin, lingering first at her throat, then plunging into her hair to hold her steady. His arms of tempered steel kept her close and safe. His hard chest crushed against her breasts. As her hips arched into his, his rigid cock brushed against her clit.

A low moan caught in her throat as he pumped his hips the slightest bit, giving her a taste of what might come if they took this erotic scenario a little farther. Her clit ached and Synna arched her hips, wanting that heated pressure. If he didn't put her out of her misery soon, she didn't know what she'd do. She hadn't masturbated in a long while, her needs submerged under work and other activities. Now, long dormant desires battled for a place inside her, refusing denial.

He allowed his hands to slide down until he cupped her ass. He gave a squeeze, and it served to remind her about their location. She pulled back from the kiss, but he kept his hands around her butt cheeks.

"Your secretary will be here soon," she said, trying to catch her breath.

He groaned and put his forehead against hers. "Damn it. You're right. We've got to stop."

With a last, lingering kiss, Ian withdrew his embrace and paced away from her until he looked like a man with a mission. A very businesslike, nonsexual mission.

"I'll…uh…" She cleared her dry throat. "I'll wait to hear from Dorky."

He nodded, and she reached around to open the door. Her heart raced and her nerves jangled so much she fumbled with the doorknob before she remembered she'd locked it. After she unlocked it, and without giving a backward glance, she left his office.

His secretary wasn't at her desk yet, thank goodness. Self-consciousness spilled over Synna as she wondered if anyone could tell from her mussed hair and well-kissed lips that she'd been snuggling with the head of SIA.

That concept ran around in her head as she continued walking, anxious to put as much distance between her and Ian's disturbing presence as possible. She couldn't fight her way out of a paper bag right now. Moments later, she arrived at a restroom near her division, and she went inside.

What she saw in the mirror reassured her. She didn't look like she'd been rolling around in bed with Ian, though her eyes held an agitated stare, her tresses a windblown scatter, and kissing had slam-dunked her lipstick.

She stared at her reflection in dismay. "What are you getting yourself into?"

She sighed and decided she'd better head to the medical area and get that test Ian had suggested, to make sure Tyler hadn't compromised her system. Fear darted across her nerves, making her jumpy and concerned.

As she left the restroom, she used the memory of Ian's hot kiss to ease her fears.

* * * * *

Cornering Tyler in the employee lounge ranked up there with one of the hardest things Synna had done. It had practically taken a presidential mandate to find a time to call him without Heidi listening in on the conversation. When Synna reached him and asked to meet somewhere private, his tone came across reluctant and grudging. She broke through his unwillingness by admitting it pertained to the Halloween party.

She arrived in the employee lounge first, her stomach jumping with nerves and her muscles strung tight thinking about what she'd agreed to do. Apprehension ran high now that she knew Tyler wasn't one hundred percent human. She'd have to fake interest so she wouldn't recoil in revulsion being near him. If he tried to hold her by dancing or anything else…well, she'd have to deal with it.

Tyler walked in a good ten minutes late, and she figured he meant it as a jab for her brush-off yesterday.

His long-sleeved white Oxford shirt, pocket protector bursting with pens, and ragged blue dress pants screamed quintessential geek. A geek demon. Who would imagine it? The knowledge almost made her snort with laughter.

He nodded and walked toward her. "Hey, Synna."

"Thanks for agreeing to meet me."

He leaned one hip against the counter, his arms crossed and his mouth turned down in a petulant frown. She wanted to smack the ridiculous expression off his face. At least he couldn't read her mind.

She plastered on a sincere smile. "I apologize for overreacting yesterday when you asked me to the party." She shrugged. "Getting ready to turn over this job to Heidi is stressful and complicated. I thought about it and realized it would be a lot of fun to go with you. So if the offer still stands…"

Tyler eyes widened to dumbstruck status. His eyes took on a surreal glow that moved through his eyes and then disappeared.

A silly grin materialized, growing slow and steady until it became his usual wiseacre smile. "Awesome. I'd love it."

Wow. That was too easy.

"Gosh, I can't believe this," he said.

Tyler cruised toward her, his attention fixed on her in a way that sent a shiver right through her frame. She didn't move, determined he wouldn't see her apprehension.

"Thanks for giving me another chance," he said.

She didn't think she could inject too much enthusiasm, so she nodded and hoped he wouldn't come closer. His familiar spicy aroma came on too strong.

His dark hair looked sprayed to his head. The strong angular bones in his cheeks and jaw reminded her of a thin boy model in a magazine for high-priced designer menswear. A sharp nose and genuinely cold almond-shaped eyes gave him an exotic appeal. Some women might find him harshly beautiful. Not her. Contrasted against Ian's rugged sensuality, Tyler lost hands down. She wished Ian stood here now instead of this man-demon.

"Something wrong?" Tyler tilted his head to one side.

"No." She clasped her hands in front of her, feeling like a prim schoolgirl under his devouring gaze.

And he did devour.

With lazy, long sweeps, his intrusive gaze didn't have the same effect on her as one of Ian's appraising looks. Tyler's attention made her feel…dirty. Touched in places with unclean flesh.

A throbbing in her temples, which hadn't responded to pain relievers, decided it would flare. A crawling need to run gathered in the pit of her stomach and tightened her muscles until she wanted to leap from her skin.

Keeping her expression calm, she said, "There are rules we need to follow tomorrow night."

A disappointed twist to his mouth said what he believed. "Rules?"

"We can't hang with each other the whole night. We should dance and mingle with others."

He shrugged. "Works for me."

Gratified, she pushed onward. "No grabbing me and kissing like you did yesterday."

For an agonizing moment, he didn't answer, and she wondered if he would change his mind about the date. "Fair enough." He jammed his hands in his pockets. "I didn't like the way Frasier threw his weight around yesterday. It wasn't his business if we wanted to kiss."

Oh brother. She almost contradicted him and pointed out that "we" didn't come into the equation. "Let's forget yesterday and start fresh. I've got to go."

She moved passed him, but he clasped her arm. "Wait. What time should I pick you up?"

Oh yes. How could she forget that? Being trapped in a car with him didn't appeal, but she couldn't think of a reasonable refusal. "The party starts at seven, so six-thirty should be enough time. I live just down the pass."

After giving him her address, she hurried away, unwilling to spend another minute in close proximity.

* * * * *

After lunch, Heidi settled in the extra chair near Synna's desk. With sparkling eyes and a teasing grin, Heidi looked ready to laugh.

"I don't think you should wear that wench outfit Halloween night," Heidi said.

Synna's concentration on the computer disappeared. Déjà vu made her hesitate, and her thought processes went into slow motion. She'd been down this road too many times in her life, and now it appeared again. The challenge reared up and bit her in the ass. She felt like a child ordered what to do, a peon under a supervisor's imperial thumb.

Synna returned to looking at the chart on the computer. She held steady. "I'm wearing it."

Synna glanced at her coworker. Did disappointment flash through those deep brown eyes? Anger? Maybe both.

"I don't think you should wear the costume," Heidi said again.

Oh great. Well, what did she expect? Pushy individuals don't stop after being smacked down once.

Synna kept her glance glued to the computer screen. "Would you like to wear a wench costume? I don't think anyone would object if we both wore one."

Heidi laughed gently, as if she'd had time to recover from Synna's parlay. "I'm wearing a gypsy costume. I wouldn't be caught dead in a wench outfit. You couldn't pay me enough. Besides, Ian will probably think it is inappropriate. Slut city."

Synna almost succumbed, almost allowed the snarky tone in the other woman's voice to make her flinch. "Hard to say what he thinks, but I don't really care."

Hold on. Hold on a little longer, and she'll leave me alone.

"Well, it's your neck." Heidi's voice held an unusual menace, but Synna didn't look her way.

Synna wouldn't give away her power. She'd conquered a little piece of her insecure past and put it where it belonged forever.

When she heard Heidi leave, she kept her gaze pinned to the computer. She didn't see anything, and her heart pounded in her ears. Now all she had to do was survive a weredemon on Halloween night.

The phone rang and made her jump. She picked up the receiver and spoke quietly. "Synna MacDell, Division Two."

"Synna." Ian's smooth, deep voice purred in her ear.

Startled but pleased, she said, "Ian. H-hi."

"Did Tyler say he'd go with you to the party?"

"Yes."

He sighed. "Good. I was afraid he might say no after your initial rejection."

"Me, too."

An awkward silence covered the line between them until she spoke. She modulated her voice to almost a whisper. "Something strange is going on, though."

"Like what?"

"Heidi said I shouldn't wear my wench costume."

"Why would she say that?"

"I don't know. I thought it was very odd."

"You don't like Heidi very much, do you?"

"It's not actually dislike. She wears me out. I'm quieter, more introspective. She's so extroverted it gives me hives."

His laugh sent a hot flare of desire into her stomach. "That bad?"

"It's hard to explain." She wanted him to understand, and she took a big risk opening up to his scrutiny. Intuition told her that Ian needed to know who she was now, not in some future that may or may not exist. Only now meant anything.

"I'm listening," he said.

"She's assertive and that isn't a bad thing, but she verges on aggressive. She's a hard worker and knows what she's doing."

"Those sound like assets."

"They are. She's also the type of person I have trouble with over and over again. It's a pattern in my life to run into aggressive women who feel they have to mold me into this image of who they believe I should be." On a roll, she continued. "They-they want me to be something I'm not because it's their vision."

"Women who want to mother you, in other words?"

"An interfering mother, not a sincere one with a willingness to let their child be who they really are."

"Damn, that sounds a lot like a description of my Grandmother Henderson."

"So you understand how it is. Once in a while life brings these bombastic women into my range. It's like the universe is testing me to see if I have the confidence to recognize the difference between my will and others'. You know when you get those little moments in your life where someone pushes your limits, you come through, and you're genuine to yourself? I have to remember who I am at that moment. Not who other people want me to be or think I am."

"Yeah." Soft and husky, his voice comforted her. "The woman I'm interested in is the one I know now. The woman you're becoming every day."

Joy surged inside her as a new flood of affection for him warmed her soul.

He sighed. "Ever get those times when you react to a situation in a way that hacks you off? You're fifteen again instead of thirty-six?"

"That's exactly it. You're an adult, and there you are succumbing to some frustration you haven't endured in a million years. It's maddening. But I have a difficult time imaging you uncertain."

"Huh. Keep your illusions about me. It makes me feel more invincible that way."

A laugh slipped through her, a new happiness.

"You know she won't make it in your position with that attitude," he said.

Synna nodded. "Oh, she will. Plenty of people like Heidi work in places of power. It's one of the reasons they make it in the world."

"You don't believe in karma?"

"I do."

"Then believe me, at some point she'll get hers. Maybe not today or tomorrow, but someday."

Synna didn't say that she wouldn't see that day before she left SIA.

"Did you get a report back from the medical lab yet?" he asked.

"Not yet. They did say they'd try to have it today, though."

"Good."

"Ian, what-what would happen if I was…if the results came out bad?"

His silence made her nervous. Finally, he spoke. "Nothing is going to happen to you. I'll make damned sure of that. Even if you were compromised by Tyler, there are ways to reverse the process."

"I can't feel relieved yet."

"Call me the minute you find out, all right?" His voice held concern.

"Of course."

His concern warmed her all the way to the bottom of her heart, and when they hung up, the glow didn't leave.

* * * * *

"I hate to say it," Dorky said over the phone to Synna not long before quitting time. "I just received your lab results and it is all true. You've got to have sex to remove the weredemon blood taint inside you."

The words echoed in Synna's head, a proclamation akin to a hanging sentence. It sounded so final. She wanted to declare Dorky batty and hang up, but the announcement left her speechless.

Less than thirty minutes ago, the medical lab called Synna and told her she'd been compromised by Tyler's kiss. Her treatment was sex. Not a simple kiss, but full on intercourse. Synna had sat, stunned, unable to form a coherent thought for almost ten minutes. Now, Dorky called and reported the same thing.

"There's something else," Dorky said, "and I'm pretty sure you aren't going to like this part."

Synna moaned. "There's more?"

Dorky sighed. "Yes. In order to inoculate you against the weredemon, the intercourse has to be unprotected."

Synna blinked. "What? What did you just say?"

Dorky cleared her throat. "You can't use birth control of any kind. You see, it isn't intercourse specifically that protects you against a weredemon. Ian's semen has to…um…come inside you. You must make love more than once to assure inoculation. Flesh-to-flesh contact."

Synna's throat seemed to close up. She couldn't catch her breath. No. No, this couldn't be true. Someone had made a terrible mistake. She glanced up and Heidi was still lurking in the cubicle. She couldn't very well blurt out her objection with Heidi standing within hearing distance.

"Are you okay?" Dorky's concerned voice asked.

Synna's mind raced for a way to ask questions.

"I'm great." Synna kept her voice low but cheerful. "Do you mean I have to…uh…complete this action just minutes before the party?"

"No. Some time between now and the party."

"Oh God."

Heidi looked up and peered at Synna, and Synna realized how desperate she sounded.

"Oh, that's good," Synna said for effect. "Very good."

"I've already told Ian." Humor leaked through Dorky's tone.

Synna's fingers tightened on the telephone receiver. "What did he say?"

"He wants you to meet him at his home tonight at six o'clock to take care of the situation."

Take care of the situation. Nothing she'd heard before about sex ever sounded so cold and clinical. Robot mechanical. A mere tab A into slot B affair.

Slow burning anger flamed within Synna. She made a command decision. She didn't care if refusing Ian's request landed her in the hottest lava since Mount St. Helen's last blew its stack. She'd been out of her gourd to agree with him, to hold him, to kiss him. Horniness had mucked up her common sense.

Point-blank, she didn't do impersonal and unprotected sex with powerful executives on a moment's notice.

"Synna? Are you there?"

"Dorky, could you do me a favor?"

"If it's not illegal and within reason."

"P-Please tell him I won't be available."

Dorky didn't make a peep at first. Soft and cajoling, she said a few seconds later, "You mean you won't be dating Tyler or you're not available for the assignation tonight?"

If she hadn't been pissed off, Synna would have found the word assignation charming and old-fashioned. "Tonight. I'm not available tonight."

A metallic clang came over the phone. "Oops, sorry. I almost stabbed myself with the letter opener. You know, Ian would have called you himself, but he has a Level Ten meeting right now."

"It's not that."

"Then what is it? Tyler is a dangerous creature. If he tries to kiss you again and keeps the kiss going long enough, you'll be in severe trouble. Having sex with someone else will inoculate you."

She glanced around the cubicle, wishing Heidi would leave so she could say what she really meant. "I'll be at the party Halloween night. That's it."

"With Tyler?"

"Yes."

Dorky's sigh held resignation. "If it's any consolation, Ian is as worried about this as you are. He knows there's a risk of getting you pregnant, and that isn't something to take lightly. Ian is healthy, so you don't have to worry about disease, and we know you're healthy from your test results."

"I can't. I won't expose myself to the risk of…" She couldn't say it.

Risk of falling for Ian? Of becoming pregnant with his child? Or both?

"I know this is a bit of a shock," Dorky said.

Synna snorted. "Just a bit."

"Please, Synna, believe me when I tell you Ian is very anxious about this situation. His primary concern is you."

Heidi left the cubicle with a stack of papers, and tension seeped from Synna's tight shoulders. She lowered her voice to a small thread.

What would it be like to have a hunky man like him worried about her wellbeing? "He hardly knows me."

If it was possible to read minds, she could have sworn Dorky's voice floated into her head. *He knows all about you. Everything.*

Mild panic nipped at her heels. Now she'd started hallucinating along with everything else.

Synna's glance darted around the cubicle, but she didn't really see anything. Instead, she remembered the two spine-melting kisses she'd experienced with Ian. Sexual attraction didn't amount to long-lasting compatibility. Practicality came before passion. She refused to let her libido dictate her next move.

And pregnancy was too damned risky to allow one night of passion.

"Please just tell him what I said," Synna said.

Dorky's normally polite tone hit a harder note. "You can't tell him yourself?"

"I've got meetings the rest of the day, then I'm heading home."

A dull throbbing in Synna's temples threatened to burst into full flower.

"I'll tell him it's a no-go for tonight and let him take it from there."

Relief flooded Synna. "Thank you. I owe you one."

Dorky's chuckled softly. "Yes, you do. One thing before you hang up. If I were you, I'd reconsider. All this may seem quick, artificial and unnecessary, but isn't your life worth more?"

Feeling prickly, Synna responded with a slightly louder voice. "I find it difficult to believe there isn't an alternative."

"Believe me, if there was another option that would guarantee the weredemon couldn't possess you, I would have told you and Ian."

Synna couldn't fault Dorky's knowledge. Cloistered in the subbasement library, the woman never saw light. At least the rumors said she didn't leave the SIA complex. No one knew why. Some considered it an urban legend, a cachet designed to make the genius research librarian seem infallible.

Footsteps sounded in the background, as if Dorky might be pacing. "You think Ian just wants to sleep with you."

A hot flush stole over Synna's face. "Yes."

"Do you want my honest opinion?"

"All right."

"Ian has Grade-A integrity. He is a big, tough guy with brawn and brains mixed into one splendid package. Women don't love him just because he's gorgeous. He's got personality and compassion. And he's honest. He wouldn't be head of SIA if he wasn't."

Synna processed the information, but she didn't trust. "I appreciate you telling me this."

"But it doesn't change your mind?"

"No. Getting involved like that isn't wise without friendship first."

Dorky's laugh tinkled quietly, a well-modulated and simple sound both pleasant and reassuring. "Who says we always have to be wise? I've made a few strange choices in the name of love."

"L-love?" The word came out on a croak, and Synna coughed and reached for her tumbler of water. After a long sip, she cleared her throat. "What has that got to do with this situation?"

"I've probably said way too much, but what the hell? Ian is wildly attracted to you. Anyone can see that. If I'm not mistaken, the feeling is mutual."

Synna rubbed her cold fingers over her forehead. "I don't think it's mutual."

Dorky's little noise of contempt for Synna's statement came through loud and clear. "Have it your way. I'll let you go so you can take care of that headache. Just give what I said some consideration. It may seem highly unorthodox, but it may save your life to…uh…have sex with Ian."

The touch of embarrassment in Dorky's voice made Synna grin. "All right. I'll think about it."

When Synna hung up the phone, she realized that somehow Dorky knew about her headache. She'd either seen her on a camera, or the woman must be psychic.

Conflicting emotions bounced around inside Synna. Ian was a major-league hottie, and she admired him so much. But having unprotected sex with him was irresponsible.

Two alternatives stared her in the face and she didn't like either one of them.

Maybe get dead. Maybe get pregnant.

Her periods were so totally irregular that she could get pregnant at any time. Taking birth control pills wasn't an option because of side effects she'd experienced in the past.

Okay, correction. Three alternatives.

Maybe find her heart broken.

Her headache flared. What was she going to do?

She was screwed…literally and figuratively.

Chapter Six

ଚଚ

Synna jerked straight out of her half doze as the doorbell rang that evening. Wiping sleep from her fuzzy brain, she sat up on the burgundy leather couch and stared at the front door. The television played digital music, a soothing New Age piece that had lulled her to sleep. Dazed by the low-intensity headache still plaguing her skull, she stared at the door like an idiot. The doorbell clanged again and trepidation made all her muscles clench. She had a feeling Ian stood outside the door. After all, she hadn't called him and said nonchalantly that she would have sex with him.

She'd decided before she fell asleep that she couldn't have sex with him this way, under pressure, under the threat of a theory on what may happen with Tyler.

Forcing her way to her feet, Synna crossed to the door and turned on the porch light. A quick look through the peephole confirmed Ian stood on the porch of her tiny Victorian home, those telltale frown lines between his eyebrows.

Anxiety, exasperation and most scary of all, excitement filtered through her emotions. He looked delicious, as he always did, and her heart did a dance of happiness.

After she unlocked the door and opened it, his expression didn't brighten one iota.

"Are you okay?" He stepped closer, anger and worry mixing in his voice. "You aren't answering the phone, and your answering machine isn't on."

"I turned the phone off."

"Are you all right?" He glanced into the room behind her, as if he expected to see a wild man standing behind her holding her hostage.

"Yes, I'm fine." She stepped back. "Come in."

As he entered and closed the door against the chill, his gaze slipped over her ruby flannel pajamas and matching fleece robe. "Having an early night?"

Heat pinked her cheeks. "Y-you've caught me in my frumpy pajamas."

He still didn't appear amused. "We all have crap pajamas somewhere in the closet."

His reassurance brought an uneasy grin to her lips. "Thanks."

Ian closed his eyes and a muscle moved in his jaw. "I didn't mean to imply—"

"It's okay. I know what you meant."

When he opened his eyes, Synna perused him as thoroughly as he had surveyed her. His hair tumbled in mild disarray over his shoulders, and the two-day stubble on his jaw gave him a hard, dangerous edge she found undeniably thrilling. A beat-up brown bomber jacket graced his broad shoulders, various macho military patches dotting the surface. Hs faded jeans curved over firm thighs. As usual, the man looked good enough to eat.

"I crashed on the couch and fell asleep," she said.

"How's your headache?" His gentle tone, matched with his caressing gaze, melted her from the inside out.

"It's getting a little better."

A rueful grin erased a little of the intensity in his eyes. "And I woke you up? I'm sorry. I was worried when you didn't answer the phone."

She couldn't deny his anxiety over her satisfied her in a wholly female way. "I didn't mean to worry you."

"We need to talk."

"I'll take your jacket."

As he handed the jacket to her, the scent of man and leather added to her already humming arousal. God, it didn't take much for him to turn her on. Toss a glance in her direction, smile, and damn it she was a Grade-A goner.

She shuffled down the hall to the closet. "Can I get you something to drink?"

"No, thank you."

Once she deposited his garment and returned, she found him still standing, taking in the small, traditionally furnished living room. His reflection showed in the large mirror above the fireplace mantel.

"Some people don't like it," she said.

He glanced her way. "What?"

"The furniture. They say it's too dark and heavy. Too Victorian. Since this *is* a Victorian, I think it's perfect. Besides, I inherited most of it from my grandmother after she died. It's a good thing, too. No one else in my family wanted it."

She almost said, *No one else gave a shit*, but she modulated her word choice.

"As long as you like it, what does it matter what anyone else thinks?" he asked.

She smiled, appreciating his statement. "Are you always so perceptive?"

"Usually. I'm very good at figuring out what is going on in someone's head, sometimes even before they know it themselves."

"You're telepathic?"

"I don't have paranormal abilities. Many of the soldiers in my unit did, but not me. There's this buddy of mine from the unit, T.J., who can do some pretty incredible things."

"Such as?"

"I can't talk about the particulars."

"Uh-huh. Why doesn't that surprise me?" Well, she wasn't *that* interested in other men at the moment. Curiosity about this virile, intriguing male superseded other concerns for this small space in time. "Have a seat."

He settled on the couch, his forearms propped on his thighs and hands clasped together as he leaned forward. When she sat next to him, she detected tension flowing off him in waves. She sensed he wanted to discuss sex, but she needed more. As overwhelmingly attractive as she found him, she hungered to know the man inside who intrigued her from the first day she saw him.

"Tell me about your time with Alpha Unit." She shrugged. "Unless it's all classified."

Surprise entered his eyes. "There's a lot I can tell you, but I'm not sure you'd want to hear it. Besides, that isn't what I came here—"

"I know why you came here."

He paused, his gaze steady and unperturbed. "Do you?"

"Yes." She shifted on the couch and leaned a little closer to him. He inhaled deeply, and a wild thrill dashed through her that maybe she did affect him strongly. She wondered if he could smell the soft rose scent in her body wash. "You want to talk about the conversation I had with Dorky earlier today."

"We need to get this cleared up now."

"I've got conditions before this conversation can go any further."

Skepticism hardened his features. "Conditions?"

"Right now, I want to know more about Ian Frasier, the soldier and the man."

He sat back against the couch, his big hands on top of his thighs in a gesture imperial and abounding with male animal. An emerald green ribbed turtleneck caressed his athletic torso and showed off his fine muscles without being too tight. Her pulse picked up speed as his thighs sprawled open in typical male ease. Shamelessly, her glance darted over the large bulge between his legs and the carved muscle in his thighs. Damn, if he didn't look delicious and undeniably masculine. She almost licked her lips. She realized she'd been staring, and her gaze snapped up to his.

"What do you want to know?" he asked.

"What makes it necessary to have Alpha Unit go in and take care of bad guys when the SIA is there to do the same thing?"

A smile eased over his lips, as if he couldn't help relax. "You know how it is, the spook agencies always need military backup."

She nodded. "That makes sense. What are your talents, if you don't have any paranormal abilities?"

He pushed up the sleeves on his sweater and exposed the darker hair on his forearms that matched his growing beard. A big black watch graced his left wrist, one of those all-purpose, waterproof to the deepest depths gadgets. "I'm a good logistics man, and before I got into Alpha Unit I was in a regular Army Special Forces unit. I'm a weapons expert, and I know several languages fluently. I attended several courses on international relations, and I've been in just about every country on earth."

"Whoa," she said softly. "Several languages?"

"Russian, Arabic, German, French, Italian, Serbo-Croatian, all three Goidelic Gaelic languages and all four Brythonic Gaelic languages."

"Holy mustard," she whispered. "I'm impressed."

He shrugged. "A few of the guys spoke more languages than me."

Doubly awed by his modesty, she asked, "Why on earth would you need to learn Gaelic languages?"

"You'd be surprised how many unearthly creatures from the Shadow Realm are of Celtic origin."

"Manx is a dead language. Cornish and Gaulish aren't used any longer."

His body seemed to relax, as if her segue away from his real reason for being here helped ease his tension. "Few people know that."

"You'd be surprised what I know about Gaelic. I know that Manx, Scottish and Irish are Goidelic and Welsh, Cornish, Breton and Gaulish are Brythonic."

"How did you learn so much about it?"

"Dorky. It's amazing what that woman knows," she said.

He nodded. "In the Shadow Realm many old things are still practiced, including languages dead in our world."

"The more I learn about this Shadow Realm, the more I want to know."

"You'll probably discover *more* than you want at the Halloween party."

"Are you trying to discourage me from asking questions?"

A laugh rumbled up from his broad chest and made her long to reach out and touch him. She wanted to lead him away from talking about sex, but suddenly she couldn't think of anything else.

He winked. "Yeah, maybe I am. In this case, innocence is bliss."

Maybe he wouldn't relinquish more information tonight, and perhaps she didn't want to know. Any additional information and maybe she wouldn't be interested in helping the SIA with Tyler anymore.

She switched gears. "Dorky is a fascinating woman."

Humor danced in his eyes. "She sure is."

The pure admiration in his tone made Synna just the tiniest bit green. Yes, Ian was attracted to Synna on a sexual level, but she longed for a connection more enduring and meaningful. Doing him, as Heidi suggested, wouldn't be enough.

"Learning Gaelic isn't an easy thing, and neither is Russian. I'll bet your IQ is pretty high, too," she said.

"Above average, yes." He said it without boasting, a certainty like the sky being blue and the earth being round.

"I'm intrigued that you went from a job in Alpha Unit to the SIA. The military wasn't exciting enough for you?"

With a laconic grin he said, "Actually, it was a different kind of excitement. I'm fascinated by the paranormal. Always have been. Short of quitting the Army and forming my own ghost hunters group, joining SIA was the best way to get a piece of the action."

"You did more than join, you run it. Somehow, I think a ghost hunter group would be too sedate for you. What I don't understand is why you didn't apply for an agent position where you would be on assignment. As the head of SIA you're stuck at the desk most of the time."

She sensed rather than saw a change in him. His eyes saddened. "I like the action, but my body and mind are weary of the constant physical and emotional work. As head of SIA I'm still a part of the team, still making key decisions."

"Wait a minute. You're fully involved in this assignment against Tyler."

A sensual smile curved his mouth in a delicious way she absorbed into her memory forever. When she left the SIA for good, she probably wouldn't see him again. The idea saddened her more than she wanted to think about.

"I'm involved because I don't want anything to happen to you, Synna, and I'm going to make damned sure nothing does."

His gaze caressed her, drinking her in with hot appreciation.

Silence washed over them and it made her nervous. She stood abruptly. "I-I think I need a brandy. I've got some up in the cabinet."

She retreated to the kitchen, thankful for the breather. The man was so tempting, so consuming she wanted to kiss him, lick him, devour him from end to end. She had to master her runaway feelings.

He followed her. "Why do I get the feeling that what I said made you nervous?"

She stopped in the middle of the kitchen, and he almost ran into her. Without answering him, she veered toward the pantry and opened the highest cabinet for the squat brandy bottle she'd used for cooking.

As she gathered two brandy glasses and then poured a measure in each glass, he continued. "Synna? Answer me."

She handed him a brandy. "Have a taste. It's really good."

He put the glass down on the counter and took a step forward. She eased back against the counter and he planted his hands on either side of her.

When he spoke, his voice came out low and non-threatening, his sensual tone caressing her nerve endings. "I could say I'm your boss, and you're required to answer me, but that's not why I'm asking. Talk to me."

"T-this whole situation with Tyler is making me apprehensive."

"I'm not going to let him hurt you."

She shook her head. "I know. I honestly believe if anyone could protect me, you could." She smirked and gave a little laugh. "You'd confound him long enough with all the languages you speak, then take him down with a karate chop."

"I don't want it to come to that."

"So what are you going to do when you catch him?"

"Bag 'em with an electrical converter sword."

"I've heard of them, but I've never seen one."

"They're wicked enough to deal with most of the creatures from the Shadow Realm, with a few exceptions. You'd be amazed at how effective they are on weredemons. Freaks them out long enough to tranquilize them."

"What happens then?"

"We put him in a special chamber designed for demons. They're carted off to the Shadow Realm and locked out of our world."

She shook her head, fascinated. "That's amazing. God, all this time I worked for the SIA and didn't know we dealt with the supernatural on this complex a level. Now I'm going to get up close and personal with it."

"Not that close if I can help it. Now tell me what else is wrong. It isn't just the assignment making you skittish as a cat."

Go ahead, Synna. Blurt it out. "I'm not changing my mind about having sex with you, but I know that's why you came here tonight."

"I was worried about you. As far as the sex situation, you could be hurt or killed by Tyler if things go wrong."

She ignored the fact he stood so close, his arms caging her up against the counter. "So you're saying if I have sex with you or someone else, neither of those things can happen?"

His eyes narrowed. "Of course not, but if he kisses you again, you could be hurt. Is that what you want?"

"No." The one syllable sounded whispery and desperate.

"Your system was already compromised by that damned kiss Tyler gave you. Did medical tell you that's why you have the headache?"

Startled, she stared at him. "No."

"That's why you aren't feeling too well. It can act on your system like a low-grade infection." He reached up and placed his big palm against her forehead. "Damn, you're a little warm."

She did feel hot, but she figured his proximity had more to do with it than weredemon bugs.

Without waiting for her to reply, he said, "Sex with a full human is the only way to be somewhat certain he can't mate with you." He reached down and took her hands in his palms. More warmth raced from where he touched her into all corners of her body. "You're driving me crazy, Synna."

She felt cheeky and took a chance. "Because I'm not doing what you want?"

"Yeah." His mouth quirked in amusement. "You're a little stubborn."

She sniffed and eased away from his grip on her hands and the closeness of his body. "Really? And you're not? How much respect would you have for me if I'd buckled under to this sex-on-demand idea?"

He groaned in apparent frustration. "It's not sex-on-demand, it's sex because we both want it and because—"

"It's a solution to a major problem."

Ian planted his hands on his hips. "Yeah, to put it bluntly."

Dissatisfaction mingled with scorching hunger in his eyes. Synna thrilled as she put him on the edge, and she stepped into clearly dangerous territory. Excitement climbed inside her.

"Ian, it isn't just the sex and you know it."

He nodded solemnly. "Yeah, when Dorky told me I had to come inside you, I about flipped my lid."

Come inside you.

It sounded so intimate. The ultimate in giving, in accepting. A wild thrill tingled in her belly and shot down between her legs. Whether she wanted it to or not, the idea of his bare cock moving inside her, caressing her deep and spewing hot semen into her—

Oh shit. Her belly fluttered with nerves, and her heart picked up speed. Her mind rebelled but her body loved the idea of him inside her. Naked. Thrusting hard and fast.

She drew in a slow breath. "The risk is too much. You could get me pregnant, and I'm not ready for that responsibility."

He nodded. "For your safety it's something that can't be helped."

She glared at him. "There has to be another way to solve this."

His eyes looked sad. "Synna, you know I wouldn't leave you alone with a baby. If you got pregnant, I'd take responsibility. I'd be a father to the child."

A wild little image flew through her mind. Ian holding a newborn with love in his eyes. Yes, she could imagine him loving the child they made together, but he didn't love her. The last thing she wanted was a child born without the parents in a committed and loving relationship.

"It's not just the idea of becoming pregnant, is it?" His breathing came a little quicker as his chest moved up and down. "Are you frightened by what you feel and the fact we've kissed?"

"Of course. If you were me, wouldn't you be a little concerned?"

"Hell, yes." He slipped his arms tightly about her waist and yanked her close. One of his hands rode dangerously close to her ass. "I'd wonder if the man with his arms around me just wanted to get into my pants when he's known me a very short time, when he doesn't know as much about me as I think he should."

"Do you want to know me?" A little sadness lurked around the exhilaration of being in his arms. "Really know me?"

"Of course. Body and soul. You said that you trusted me, but it sounds like you don't."

She shook her head. "I want to."

He gave her a killer grin that made her heart ache. "You're going to make me wait, aren't you?" He laughed gently and buried his face in her hair. "God, I want you. I've never wanted a woman as much as you."

She almost groaned. She'd started to fall hard for him and didn't know if his feelings went as deep.

Damn it all, she would get it out in the open and hope for the best. "What do you feel for me?"

He didn't flinch at the question. His gaze went lambent and furnace hot. "That's easy. The first day I saw you I was intrigued, then every time we met after that, I wanted to know more and more. I want to know about your life — why you've got that cute little stutter."

Her eyes widened. "Cute? I haven't stuttered in years. I got over it as a teenager, but the stress lately with this weredemon stuff and you—"

"Me?" He grinned. "I make you stutter?"

"Yes. Sometimes. I'm…whenever I get nervous, even just a little, I stutter. I've worked a lot of years to get rid of it and now it's back."

"I'm sorry."

She frowned. "I'll get rid of it again."

"I'm sure you will." He stared at her for a long time before he continued. "I made sure I went to lunch at twelve every day no matter what the hell was going on just to see you. You could say I've got a major hard-on for you and it isn't going away."

She laughed. "Now that's the first time a man has ever said that to me."

"You've got to be kidding? Are all the men around here insane?" Unrelenting, he caught her gaze and held steady. "Were you embarrassed when Dorky told you that you have to have sex as a precaution?"

She sighed. "Yes. Sex as a precaution. Unprotected sex, no less. That's a hell of a note."

He cupped her face tenderly in a way that made her heart flutter. His callused fingers felt protective as he brushed his thumbs over her cheeks. "I decided I'd convince you that you do have to have sex before the party. And that you shouldn't have that sex with anyone else but me."

Chapter Seven

ဢ

Ian's statement shouldn't have surprised Synna, but the absoluteness made her pause. His gaze took her in with sweltering intensity, searching her eyes for the answer. She didn't know another man she could have sex with, and confessing it would sound pathetic. Ian alone piqued her interest.

"Why do you care if it's anyone else?" she asked.

"Damn it, Synna, it should be clear by now." He drew away and scowled. "Hell. I'm taking this too fast. The last thing I want is to frighten you."

Ian grabbed for his brandy glass, tipped it to his lips, and finished it in one gulp. He placed the glass down on the counter.

"No," she said. "You don't frighten me. It's not..." The words stalled, her throat aching with tension.

"Hey." His fingers drifted until they touched her throat. "Your pulse is going too fast. What's wrong?"

How could she explain? "I'm edgy. You scare me, all right, but not the way you think. I know you wouldn't hurt me physically."

That's it. That's what will make him turn around and run. If I tell him too much information. If I explain I can only make love with him if we have a commitment. Most men would stampede away so fast.

Her silence didn't move Ian. He stayed planted in front of her, his nearness like a brand, burning into her in a way she would still remember as an old woman.

When he opened his mouth to speak, she impulsively covered his firm lips with two fingers.

"I'm scared of letting you so far into my heart. I'm not the kind of woman who can have fun in bed with a man I barely know, Ian. My heart has to be involved."

His mouth tightened, and the rubbing of his lips under her finger pads sent curls of desire to her stomach. She pulled her hand away. God. The man could do almost nothing, nothing at all, and affect her on so many levels. Her emotions rolled from pleasure to sadness. Out of control, her body refused to take commands from common sense saying she shouldn't respond and shouldn't get involved any deeper with him or the weredemon situation. She should walk away now before her heart and mind became fully entrenched.

He reached up and trapped her fingers against his mouth, and kissed them softly. He drew her hand into both of his and held it against his chest. Exasperation etched his features into a deep frown. Good. Maybe she'd turned him off sufficiently. The satisfaction she expected to feel didn't materialize. A dull ache formed in her stomach. Silence stretched like a rubber band she feared would snap in her face.

"What are you hiding?" His voice held raw emotion, and concentrated need to understand.

"It's simple," she said in defense. "Don't tell me you've never heard of the concept of *not* sleeping around."

"Damn it, Synna." His voice went deadly soft. "I never asked you to sleep around. I asked you to have sex with *me. Only me.*"

Despite the consternation turning his eyes a deeper indigo, tenderness in his touch belied the fierceness in his eyes.

"I-I'm not who you think I am," she said.

"What do you mean?"

"I started in the SIA all those years ago because of something that happened in my family when I was young."

She pulled her hand from his and turned toward the counter and her brandy. She took a hit from her glass and savored the heat and mellow taste as it slid down her throat. Keeping her hands cupped around the bowl of her brandy glass, she turned back to him. Revealing the truth inch by inch would be harder than facing Ian's unrelenting scrutiny. The glass acted as a shield, no matter how small.

"Tell me, Synna. I'm listening."

Have I made a huge mistake?

Ian watched her eyes, their normal reserve thawing as she unleashed emotion. He might not have extraordinary psychic capabilities, but he'd always read people with ease. Tonight, Synna didn't have her guard up as well as she usually did. The signs were all there. Eyes averted to a space somewhere beyond his shoulder, her gaze took on a pensive, almost moody disposition.

"Tell me." He refused to back away until he'd unraveled her mysteries. "I need to understand."

She shook her head and her hair tumbled, a silky maple blanket around her shoulders. He wanted to touch it, to know the texture. He tightened his hands into fists at his sides.

Did her hand tremble as she took another sip of brandy? "After my father died, my mother had a breakdown. Everything went wrong. I was working at the local college as a secretary and getting my degree in Art. I let that drop to help my mother."

"Your sister didn't help?"

"No. She said she was too busy with other things. I struggled to help my mother keep my parents' printing business open. A year later Mom died, and I closed the business entirely—sold it off. I didn't crack up after my father or mother died, but when I tried to go back to my art…"

She inhaled, and her eyes became suspiciously bright. Tension seemed to draw her shoulders up higher, as if she wanted to hunch into herself and disappear. She put the brandy glass back on the counter. He cupped her shoulders and she stiffened.

Shit, he hated having this effect on her. "It's okay. Don't stop now."

Synna didn't look at him, but as he rubbed her shoulders, her delicately shaped body started to relax.

"I was a sculptor. A pretty fair one. At least the reviews were good and my professors liked my work."

"And?" He couldn't resist brushing hair away from her forehead.

"I guess I'd been away from it too long. Those months, dealing with my parents and their deaths—it drained me down to nothing. I stumbled along but couldn't return to the flow. It was like I'd never created before and didn't have the talent to start with."

Her words sounded forced, her voice strained and hurting. Her throat worked as she closed her eyes.

Ian waited, his gut and soul aching for her. "You held your grief inside trying to keep everything together for everyone else. You sacrificed until you had nothing left to give."

She opened her eyes, and when tears shimmered there, he pulled her against his body lightly. It broke him to see the pain and uncertainty in her beautiful eyes.

Rubbing her back with a cadence he hoped she found soothing, he urged her to continue. "Then the SIA came along?"

"I applied and got the job. I gave up on the career I'd wanted for something safer and more certain. I was tired of change and opening up a vein for my art."

Words and sympathy came easily. "You abandoned your art for so long."

"It wasn't my parents' death that stopped me. Don't get me wrong, I know I gave up on myself. I listened to years of training from my family. They wanted me to be practical and do what it took to make money and survive."

"You could have done it as a hobby."

She nodded. "Of course. And I knew the minute I touched that clay, I'd want to do it full-time. I'd eventually be inspired and need it like the air I breathe. Finally, a few months ago, I tried to sculpt again."

Delight and exuberance returned to her eyes as she looked up at him. Ian loved the sparkle, the undeniable joy replacing regret, and it made him want her even more. He kept his arms around her.

"It was heaven," she said. "One night I worked for five hours straight without much of a break. It was one of the best feelings I've ever experienced."

"You're quitting SIA because you want to restart the career you gave up all those years ago. Right?"

Nodding slowly, she said, "I decided to take a risk. I decided to stop wallowing in a dull certainty."

While he'd always admired her, more appreciation grew inside him. Her intellect, her tenderness, her good heart stirred his cock as well as his soul. "That's wonderful, Synna. Do you know how few people follow their dreams?"

"Yes."

Synna couldn't believe the wash of security flowing through her as she realized he really did understand her. She felt it in her bones, in her blood, in her heart.

As he drew her nearer, his voice became sensual velvet against her ears. "Whenever I'm in the same room with you I can't think of anyone or anything else. You're becoming an obsession."

Indignation mixed with awe. "Are you saying I'm keeping you from doing your job?"

"Yes and no."

Involuntarily, her fingers smoothed over his chest. "W-which is it?"

His lips trailed over her forehead, hot and gentle. "I'm so confused I don't know which way is up, Synna. I started this job full of confidence, and now you're in the picture and my world is upside down."

It took her a long time to find her next words. "You've dealt with weredemons before when you were with Alpha Unit?"

"Yes."

"Then why is this case so difficult?"

"It's not the weredemons so much. It's worrying about you and wanting you. My body goes out of control, and I want to hold you. Kiss you." He whispered in her ear. "Fuck you."

Desire sizzled along nerve endings she never realized she owned. A long, deep shiver heated her body. She must say something in last defense before his nearness and touch wiped all common sense from her head. "I've waited so long to become a sculptor. I don't want to lose that dream again."

"I know," he said tenderly. "No matter what happens, you're an artist, and that isn't going to change. You'll sculpt and enjoy the career you've always wanted. I promise you."

"How can you promise me that? How?"

"Because I won't let you give up on it. Ever. Your happiness means so much to me." Ian's breath brushed against the side of her neck as he nuzzled her, his palms sliding up and down her back with gentle pressure. "I ache inside. I thought back to the last time I felt this type of desire this strongly." He drew back and looked deep into her eyes. "You've surprised me, taken me by storm."

Dazzled by his admiration, and feeling deep down that he meant every word, her fears started to ease. She leaned into him and gathered strength and reassurance from his authoritative presence, enjoying the electricity she felt pressed along the strong, hard length of his muscles.

Hip to hip, breathing in his manly scent, she felt cared for and protected. As his lips touched her neck, she absorbed the sensual enjoyment. Her hands fisted in his sweater. The soft, springy texture and the solidness of his body comforted her.

His fingers tangled in her hair, massaging the back of her neck with gentle persistence. Heat and sincerity smoldered deep in his mysterious eyes.

"Every time I see you, my body reacts. I get a hard-on that about cuts a hole through my pants. I want to drag you off like a caveman, rip away your panties, lift you up against a wall, and fuck until I can't stand upright." Passion thickened his tone. "Then I want to get you naked, lie with you on the bed and fuck for hours."

Oh my.

Her breathing increased, her pulse racing under the onslaught of his erotic statements.

"Synna," his voice turned huskier, passion heating his tone, "you want me to tell you that I'm falling hard and fast for you? That I'm so damned upset about you being with Tyler that it makes me sick? Well, it's true."

Her heart tripped over, starting a fast beat. Feeling more than a little breathless, she slipped her arms around his neck. "My God, Ian, t-that's amazing."

His lips trailed across her cheek until they reached her right ear. Nuzzling delicate, sensitive skin, his hot breath made her quiver. "Amazing as in you can't wait to do it?"

His lips caressed her nose in a little kiss, then pressed a hotter taste to her forehead. The suggestive tone in his voice and the visuals he'd painted started a chain reaction of wildfire passion in her body. Make love for hours? Her body ached to know his, to feel a wild, screaming orgasm.

What would it be like to lie under his hard, big body and feel the thick, naked length of his cock sliding in and out? What would it be like with his cock hammering in and out of her as he took her up against the wall? Either way, the visualization sent her into a serious meltdown.

How could she deny what she must do to save herself, and what she must do to live life to its fullest in case everything on Halloween night went to hell?

She couldn't reject him again. Didn't want to reject him again.

"If that isn't what you want, if you don't feel like I do, tell me now and I'll figure out some other way to keep you safe." He raked his fingers through her hair. "But, God, I want to kiss you. I want to—"

"Shut up," she said with a smile, her body and heart decided.

She threw away last caution, his convincing statements more than enough to stave off that last hesitation.

He smiled. "What?"

"You heard what I said." She reached up, plunged her fingers into his tumble of thick hair, and drew him down for a kiss.

As his mouth plundered hers without remorse, she dove into a new, sensual world. His tongue plunged deep, ravenous and intent. Banked tension rippled in his muscles as his arms tightened around her.

She broke from the kiss, released his hair, and took his hand to lead him upstairs to the bedroom. Nerves left her, the excitement she felt overruled by languorous desire. When she reached her bedroom, she pushed the dimmer switch, then turned it to diffuse the light.

Without hesitation, she drew him toward the dark wood king-sized sleigh bed. An emerald green velvet comforter covered the high, thick mattress. Several decorative pillows added luxurious comfort. Releasing his hand, she drew back the comforter with a flick of her wrist.

She turned to Ian and reached for the zipper on her fleece robe. She paused, a self-conscious smile on her lips. "This isn't exactly the sexiest attire I've ever worn."

An answering grin, irreverent and accepting, brought good humor to his eyes. His fingers trapped hers, then gently drew them away from the zipper. "You look wonderful in anything. You could be wearing a fucking burlap sack and you'd turn me on."

She laughed softly. Before she could speak, he reached for her zipper and drew it down, down, down. The quiet sliding noise became an erotic counterpoint, an anticipation drawn tight and ready to spring loose. She pushed the robe off her shoulders and tossed it onto the foot of the bed. Next, he worked on the buttons of her flannel pajama top, his knuckles brushing against her skin. She almost held her breath, like a virgin might during her first sexual encounter. A moment ago, she'd been full of confidence, but now his touch undid her one link at a time, one heartbeat away from sex with a man she knew would bring her the most exquisite encounter she'd ever known. She ached to open to Ian, to let him know her in the most elemental way. Yet she feared what would happen and what he'd find when he reached her deepest, most buried essence.

He stopped halfway down, diving in to take a kiss. He wrapped an arm around her waist and brought her nearer. As his mouth feasted on hers, hungry and ravenous, he slipped one hand into her open flannels and cupped her breast. She moaned in soft desire as he kneaded her flesh. When he brushed his fingers over her already hard nipple, she jerked a little in his arms as heated ecstasy tightened the bud. His tongue plunged deep into her mouth as he pulled at her nipple, each tug upon sensitive flesh drawing her desire closer to culmination. He worked the tight nipple, brushing over it with his thumb, then twisting and plucking until she squirmed in his arms with unbearable desire. She pulled back from his kiss, her heart pounding fiercely.

She reached for the last button on her top. As the button came loose, he eased the garment off her shoulders and down over her wrists and fingers. He laid it over the footboard.

In the low light, his intense gaze concentrated on one feature at a time. His palms coasted over her shoulders, a slow movement with both hands as he slid down over her upper arms, then to forearms and wrists.

"Fucking beautiful," he whispered as he consumed her with his heated gaze.

She'd never been observed like this before, with the single-minded purpose of a man determined to enjoy and please. She breathed in deeply and his scent, so heady and arousing, almost made her reach for him. Waiting, as the wonderful tension heightened, felt somewhere between torture and madness and the most dazzling happiness she could imagine. Sometimes sex came on an impulse like this, unplanned and brought about by unstoppable desire. Tonight would be a quality experience of soul-wrenching completeness. It felt more than right.

She looked into his eyes often now. There she saw amazing, primitive desires rise up and swallow him.

Having him this helpless made her feel more vulnerable as well. No regrets and no holding back.

He lifted her hand and turned her palm over, then leaned in to taste her wrist. He breathed in deeply. As his breath and kiss flickered over tender skin, she shivered.

"Ian." Synna knew her voice sounded quivery. She didn't care, out of control and hanging by a small tether of restraint. "This is driving me insane."

Ian cupped her breast, and for a flash-fire second she was self-conscious. The rapt look in his sea-tossed eyes refused to let her feel inadequate.

With a groan, he leaned in and captured one nipple between his lips. She gasped as heat tingled in her breast and burst into life. He sucked, starting with soft draws of his lips, then deep pulls. He manipulated the bud with his tongue, with licks and maddening tastes. She closed her eyes and dove into sensation, her heartbeat quickening as delicious pleasure danced through her breast. She trembled in his arms, sharp need darting into her lower stomach. His hands palmed her hips and drew the flannel bottoms downward until they pooled around her ankles. He moaned and the vibration tingled in her nipple as he sucked and licked with greedy attention.

Switching to her other breast, he cupped the tender globe. She looked down at his big palm, his long fingers shaping her. Nothing prepared her for the profound tug of excitement his gentle massage brought. Her senses soared as he drew his thumb and finger upward and clasped the already hard nipple.

As he pinched the tight nipple, her lips parted on a soft moan, her delight stirring to maddening depths. He tormented with steady brushes and tugs. Every flick of his tongue, every movement of his fingers made her breathy moans come deeper, more desperate until she didn't care how she sounded or looked.

Grabbing at his waist, she worked at his belt. When her fingers trembled, clumsy with desire, he released her long enough to make short work of the buckle. As he undid it, she grabbed the hem of his shirt and dragged it upward. She drew the sweater up and over his head and lobbed it onto the end of the bed. Leaning over, he drew off his black boots. He tossed them into a corner, along with his socks. He stripped away his pants and black briefs with a few tugs and discarded them.

Oh my, my.

If ever a man described delicious, Ian did. Ian's body personified masculine beauty in her eyes. People defined handsomeness in different ways, but she knew any woman looking upon his gorgeous physique would think the same thing. His skin glowed golden, flattered and framed by the ambient light. His body promised commanding protection and shelter from the storm. What woman wouldn't love his broad shoulders, sculpted biceps and strong forearms? She'd always loved his hands. Long fingers and broad palms made masculine, strong hands. Yet their elegant design and perfect lines made them beautiful rather than ugly. And, ah. That chest. Powerful, with russet hair trailing over hard pecs and down over a six-pack stomach. Long, stalwart legs peppered with hair ended with strong feet.

The coup de grâce came in the attributes between his legs. His cock stood erect from a nest of brown hair. Thick and long, his masculinity made her mouth go dry. As she stared in total awe, his cock twitched, hardening even more, engorging with obvious excitement. His balls hung firm and large. She imagined that incredible hardness pushing deep between her legs, feeling the broad head piercing deeper and deeper until he touched her womb... *Oh God. Yes.* He'd widen her, stretch her to the limit with his girth, and she wanted to know what it would feel like more than she wanted her next breath. She licked her lips involuntarily.

Ian's gaze turned hot, burning for her and her alone. Her heart beat faster in eagerness. Other thoughts faded, worry, uncertainty, all removed. Only his obvious hunger remained.

She went into his arms and surrendered to the rising tide. As his hands settled on her back, then smoothed down over her ass, she sighed. He buried his face in her hair. Kneading and caressing, he palmed her ass as his lips coasted down over her neck and nibbled until he reached her shoulder.

Synna allowed her body to know his. Nothing else in this world felt like the, and she knew in her heart that nothing would be the same again. Her life stretched behind her, some memories good, others murky and others painful.

Friday evening she would face a weredemon in human disguise. She'd never looked for danger or craved it, yet tonight the risky future felt overlaid by a satin-smooth sensuality. Tonight she could savor a joining, despite what could happen in the days ahead.

She slipped out of his arms and onto the bed, her skin brushing against the soft sheets. She'd imagined making love on this bed before to a faceless stranger in a fantasy not so long ago. Yet her fantasies couldn't live up to the situation and the man standing before her.

She lay back, her arms akimbo, one leg straight out, the other drawn up. His gaze fixated on the area between her thighs. She opened her legs further and gave him a good view.

Ian's need quickened as her secrets were revealed to him. Under a veneer of shyness lurked a siren, a woman who called to his wishes. Lust slammed him, hard and fierce.

Her luscious pussy lips, pink, swollen and slick with her arousal, asked for his touch. He wanted to lick, to stroke, to stick his tongue far inside her. He smoothed his tongue over his lips, wanting her taste. His cock jerked as he drew in the scent of her musky excitement. God, he would feel her mystery under his tongue, his lips, his fingers. Now.

"Yes," he said. "Let me see you."

Her vaginal opening, protected by soft lips, opened like a lush fruit. Wet, soft, aroused. He fixated on the beginning cleft of her ass, and he wanted to touch her there, too. Would she allow him? Had another man possessed the tight region nestled in that deep cleft? He wanted to wipe away the memory of all other men from her mind. His cock grew more swollen at the thought of sliding into first her pussy, then her ass. He'd know her mouth, her pussy and if she'd allow it, her ass before the night finished.

Synna knew he stared at her, all of her, and she closed her eyes, unable to withstand a wave of self-consciousness. She'd felt so secure moments ago. Now her heart picked up the pace and her face flushed with heat. Excitement raced along her body, an unrelenting stimulation mixing with uncertainty. How could she be anything else? He'd barged into her world and they'd spent a little time together. Now they ventured to make love. Giving up her body to intimacy so deep felt profound, though they hadn't declared lifelong love.

She opened her eyes and took in his male beauty again, awed by a staggering need to touch him from his head to his toes.

Ian crawled onto the bed beside her, his forearm slipping under her neck. Being this close to his nakedness, the essence of what made him unique and male, halted her breath. She reached up to cup his face, his hair-rough skin rasping along her fingertips. Silky and prickly at once, the sensation sent a shiver through her body. She dared gaze into his sky clear eyes, jumping into his depths to find the truth. All she saw there was kindness and gentleness mixed with a stirring heat that threatened to boil over. His palm slipped over her stomach. He touched her, desired her. She couldn't hide.

Ian closed his eyes and traced his fingers over the smooth column of her neck, lingering and teasing the hollow. She shivered under his touch and he groaned. Yes. Damn it, yes. He wanted her complete surrender. Male needs burst forth, demanding he take control until she begged for a finish. His fingers cupped around her breast, holding the weight, testing it with kneading fingers until he clasped her nipple and tugged first one, then the other. Her moan made him smile, and he opened his eyes to look down on the woman moving restlessly in his arms as he tugged at her nipples.

Synna thought she'd go mad with wanting.

They may have started quickly, their need for lovemaking fierce, but now they'd tempered the tide. A strange hurt passed through his eyes, a vulnerability she'd seen once before the first time he'd kissed her.

"Ian, what's wrong?" she asked softly, palming his face again, then sliding down his neck and to a hard biceps.

He kissed her forehead, then her nose, then his mouth hovered within inches of hers. "I would do anything in the world to keep you from being hurt."

"Even make love to me?" A grinding uncertainty rose up and tried to remove this tender moment. "Would you...would you be here if it wasn't to try to protect me from the weredemon?"

He drew back far enough to gaze into her eyes. All she saw there was honesty and a rising passion. "God, yes I'd be here. This isn't just to keep you safe from the weredemon. Even if Tyler couldn't hurt you Halloween night, I couldn't have resisted you. I'd want to be with you."

He captured her lips under his, and the world melted into glorious commotion.

Chapter Eight

ॐ

This kiss felt different, as if Ian's declaration added the essential piece in the seduction of her senses.

Synna's body shuddered deliciously as his mouth devoured, his tongue taking possession of her mouth and stoking with carnal thrusts. Wet and aching, her body needed and demanded his. She drew in a deep, sighing breath.

This is so incredible. He is mine to touch, to cherish. Happiness gripped her, a fiery companion to the awakening drawing her deeper into his arms.

"Ian," she whispered against his neck as his kiss slipped down her neck.

"Mmm?"

"God, this is so good."

"Oh, honey, this is better than good." His voice drawled smooth and sexy into her ear. Tracing her ear with his tongue, he said, "We're going to burn this damn place down."

She felt it when he couldn't resist her, when the male in him called to the female in her and demanded fulfillment of his deepest cravings. She fell over the edge and joined him.

His touch slipped over her ass, her hips and her stomach, palming the skin until she squirmed in his hold. His kisses lingered, some fiery, others as gentle as breath. Cupping her breast, he held it for an eternity before his thumb traced over the nipple, then drew his fingers up to pinch and pluck. She writhed, tormented. Her body rioted, wanting his fire inside her. His tongue flicked over her nipple as he held the round flesh captive. Every feathery brush, every lingering lick sent quicksilver burning to her core. Hot and aching, she moved against him, searching his arms, tracing the power as his body worshiped hers. She reached until she found his firm ass and squeezed. He moaned at her touch, and she tested resilient muscle.

Ian quivered as she slipped her hands from his ass and her long fingers trailed down his stomach, then headed south. His cock twitched. She skirted his cock and cupped his balls. He couldn't stop the groan that left his throat. His thighs tightened, tension coiling in his muscles as she tested him.

He clasped her hand and urged her to encircle his cock. He gasped as she stroked. Experimental, her touch grew bolder, moving up and down his length. After only a few strokes, he trapped her hand against his firm flesh. It was too much, and his heart thudded frantically in his chest, his breathing hard.

"No more. I won't be able to take it."

Gratified by his heady response, she smiled wickedly. She loved his reaction and wanted more. What would it be like to see all this bristling masculinity lose complete control?

His thighs drew her attention next as she explored to her heart's content. Yet she stayed away from his cock, saving that treat for last.

He was hers and she his and nothing would darken this night.

His tongue swept one nipple and a startled gasp flew from her throat. He bathed her breast with long, wet licks, tasting, biting gently until the heat tortured her. He drew her nipple between his lips and sucked deep. In an agony of wanting, she groaned. Remorseless, he sucked harder on her nipple until she wriggled, a moan leaving her throat. When his fingers traced over her mons and then parted her pussy lips to find her clit, she almost came. Her vagina clenched, hovered on the verge of explosion. She couldn't take this any longer.

"Please," she whispered against his lips.

As he tutored her body, she flew with the stars, her thoughts only on their lovemaking. Warm and wet, she felt the heat building as he dipped first one finger, then two into her channel. He reached high up inside until he hit that special spot no man had touched before.

"Oh," she gasped.

He said huskily, "Tell me what you need."

"You. Only you."

"Like this?" He started a rhythm with his fingers, pushing and thrusting back and forth. His big fingers rasped against her tender walls, moving easily through the slick arousal he'd brought forth inside her. "Or do you want me to eat you?"

The hot, carnal way he asked her sent a sizzle of hot need through her entire body. "Yes."

He slipped his fingers from her and moved away, down to the V of her thighs. He sipped at wet folds, lingering over one side and then the other. His tongue darted within, pushing into her body with dips and swirls. As he fucked her with his tongue, his thumb started a gentle stroke over the hard button of her clit. She moaned, moving her hips. Years had passed since she'd taken a lover, and years had vanished since she'd felt the hot, wonderful sweep of a man's tongue between her legs. Over and over he thrust his tongue in and out, until she quivered on the brink. Panting, half out of her mind with the need to come, she whimpered.

"Please, Ian."

He parted her pussy lips, then darted his tongue over her clit. Two fingers slipped deep into her pussy and started that rhythm again. Her breathing accelerated, her heart beating a mad tempo as arousal rose to furious heights. A steady heat blossomed in her pussy, her vaginal walls tingling. Her heart, her lungs, her entire body would explode from pleasure if he didn't end her misery soon.

Animal craving, primitive and beyond words, took control of her. She pulled at his hair, tugging gently to urge him up to her.

"I need you now," she said softly, tormented with need to have him inside her.

She expected him to thrust inside her, but instead he returned to her folds. His tongue brushed relentless and certain upon her clit. He reached up and clasped her nipples, tormenting each with insistent pulls. Synna's body moved in his hold as sharp pleasure expanded in her breasts.

He stopped, and she gasped. "God, Ian."

He laughed softly and crawled up her body. Propping on his forearms, he hovered over her, his weight and heat intimidating and dominating in an age-old male bid for her body. His muscular thighs wedged between hers and the tip of his cock touched her swollen opening.

He hissed in a breath, his eyes closed. "Jesus, honey."

Husky and intense, his voice told her everything she needed to know. This man wanted her with a fierceness that would outlast any everyday concerns. What they experienced now, together, transcended hours of talk, of slow getting to know each other.

His gaze, hot with desire, pinpointed hers in the dim light. His eyes closed tightly for a moment as he moaned. "You're fire and you're burning me up."

With a single, smooth motion, he fed his cock through her folds. She gasped, startled by how much he stretched her with one thrust. Her walls expanded over his length.

Slow and steady his cock parted, then retreated, then urged deeper until his hips stirred into a gentle gyration that brought him halfway inside, then out again, then in. Each thrust sent more tingles of heavy arousal through her loins. Mindless with sensation, her body writhed, pushed, hips moving to the beat. His breath rasped against her ear as he tongued the lobe and whispered erotic suggestions that fired her into overdrive.

"Come on, fuck me," he said, his voice raw.

She responded by tilting her hips upward, trying to draw him deeper.

Again, his voice rasped against her ear. "That's it. Come on. Take me."

Lovemaking became a teasing battle between them as a tight ball of ecstasy hovered just out of her reach, drawn to a screaming fine point with each thrust of his hips. Rocking into her, he advanced and retreated with steady cadence. To Synna, it felt as if he could make love to her forever, as if the pleasure would hover on the peak for a dozen years and never let her go.

"Ian," she rasped. "Please."

"You like my cock deep inside you? Then tell me how you want it."

"Harder. Harder!"

He drew back and jammed high right where she needed it, his thrusts unmerciful.

A moan of pleasure left her throat.

Her fingers dug into his ass as the heights came closer. *Almost there. Almost.*

Pleasure burst, hot and sweet, and so stunning she couldn't breathe. A scream left her, a high-pitched ecstasy-filled groan.

He growled against her neck. "Yes!"

He pulled out of her. Before she could catch her breath, he lifted Synna's legs up over his shoulders, tilting her hips high. Bending over her, he inserted his cock just inside her pussy lips and held.

His nostrils flared, his eyes wilder, glazed with deep passion. She saw something within him, primitive and private that she knew he'd never revealed to another woman. Fierce emotion melted her heart, a combination of sadness and stunning joy.

He shoved deep, and she gasped at the exquisite pressure of his cock against her walls. In this position, he drove all the way to her womb. Again, he thrust, the tempo stroking against that pleasure spot high inside until she could no longer take the pressure. Climax reached for her, and she writhed against his plunging hips, squirming as screaming pleasure surged, then pulsated with hard ripples. As he pounded her pussy, the motion fueled her orgasm until she moaned in tormented delight.

He plunged high into her and pressed deep, grinding his cock inside. She felt his cock pulse and throb as his entire body quaked. Warmth filled her inside as he jerked and his cock released its life-giving cum. A snarl left his throat, a shout of triumph.

His weight sank against her, then he quickly rolled with her in his arms. As their breaths rasped, she sank into heaven. Warm, hard and protective, he wrapped around her like a blanket. No storm could touch her, nor unwelcome thoughts. She pushed away reality, happy and content in having this time with him.

They'd rested quietly, not even speaking. A few minutes passed, and Ian started to caress her again.

As her palms moved over his torso, he gathered her against his chest, rolled onto his back, and took her with him. This time, though…he wanted something different. He hoped she'd want it, too.

She smiled, then kissed him. Happy with her assertiveness, he plunged his fingers into her hair and held her in place. Her tongue took his mouth, and he hummed in satisfaction. Her body quivered, and it made him feel powerful and needed. He'd never wanted a woman more than he did her, and it meant pleasing her in any way she asked.

Shit, I'd jump off a fuckin' bridge for her.

Shaken to the core, he broke their kiss and looked deep into the guileless depths of her eyes.

Ian's eyes looked incredibly dark, their message untamed. She loved what she saw there, even when she couldn't be sure of everything she saw. He kissed her, his tongue plunging deep. He urged her into a duel and she took him up on the offer. She drew back from his kiss.

His cock was a hard blade against her leg, and she slid over his hips until the long, thick bar pressed against her clit. His fingers teased her labia, spreading her warmth. When his fingers, wet with her arousal, teased between her ass cheeks, she sucked in a surprised breath. He didn't stop, brushing the sensitive area until her rich cream coated her anus. The insistent rubbing over rich nerves made her moan and squirm. Hot, forbidden, totally new needs assaulted her defenses.

Gently he wormed his middle finger into her anus, dipping and retreating with tentative movements that asked for permission. He kissed her again, and his tongue thrust into her mouth, mimicking sex without reservation. Then his finger penetrated deep. Startled by the pleasure, she moaned softly into his mouth.

He moved back from her kiss and searched her gaze. "All right?"

"Yes."

He returned to kissing her, this time with gentle, searching forays. Her muscles clenched on his finger as delight tickled, itched, and demanded attention.

As his tongue pumped into her mouth, he drew his finger out, then pushed deep. Synna thought she'd go mad, the pleasure making her move her hips.

Keeping his mouth sealed to hers, he inserted two fingers into her tight opening, pushing gently. Then he worked them in and out with even, slow strokes.

He tore his mouth from hers and asked, "Do you want me here?"

Excitement rippled over skin in a long shiver at the thought. Yet she knew the answer. "Yes."

"Then you have to be more ready for this. Do you have a vibrator? Some lube?"

Heat burned her cheeks. "Um…yes."

A grin touched his lips. "Good. Because we're going to put it up your pussy while I fuck your ass."

His blunt statement caused a heat wave that reignited her sexual hunger. "Oh yes."

He released her, and she told him where to find the vibrator and the lube. Nerves threatened to derail her sexual curiosity. She'd never ventured into anal sex before, though she'd fantasized. The two lovers she'd had never suggested it, and she'd been too shy at the time to ask.

With Ian, it was right, she'd waited for *the* man and *the* perfect time. She wanted this special brand of intimacy with a surprising strength.

When he returned with the large pink dildo, she inhaled deeply with excitement.

"Turn over," he said. "We have to do this slowly. I don't want to hurt you."

His assurance eased remaining fears lingering inside her.

Gently he inserted the dildo into her pussy with a slow, steady thrust. As the dildo entered, she moaned softly.

The dildo felt tight and warm inside her, slicked by the lube. He turned the knob until a steady throbbing sent pulsating waves through her vaginal walls.

God, it felt so good, she wanted to move her hips until she found relief from the new ache. With deliberation, he inserted two lubed fingers into her anus, pushing straight and true up as high as they would go. He worked them steadily back and forth, until her hips moved with him. Her pussy hungered, clenching and releasing over the vibrating dildo. She ached for release and almost opened her mouth to beg. Her breathing went wild, ecstasy driving her to the edge.

"Come on," he said. "Feel it. Feel my fingers moving in your ass. Feel the dildo throbbing in your pussy."

Her breathing came faster and faster, heralding the hot, steady climb toward climax. Breath rasping, she reached for the heights and allowed a wave of heat to wash over her like a sea. Yes, it was building. Heightening. Almost there. Oh yes. *There.*

There.

Her body shook, her head going back on a long, high shriek as her pussy muscles clenched, then ruptured with sweet, unbearable pulses. Her breath came out in sobs as her head hung down.

"Are you ready?" he asked gently.

She nodded, wanting him inside with a powerful craving.

The dildo still pulsed. A moment later, the broad tip of his cock replaced his fingers, and with a gentle push, his cock eased through the tight opening and inside. She gasped at the slight pinch.

Holy God, he was inside her. She'd imagined more than once what it would feel like to have man's cock in her ass. She'd never known how good it could feel.

He held back. "All right? Want more?"

Guttural words slipped from her throat. "Ian. God, that feels so good."

His hands spread her butt cheeks as he withdrew, then pushed with gentle insistence until he slipped into her a short way. He withdrew and she whimpered. He spread her butt cheeks even wider, then probed her ass again with his cock. With steady, rhythmic thrusts, he pushed in and out, an inch inside at the most. The throbbing in her pussy had grown to staggering need. Filled fore and aft, her longing grew hotter and higher.

Her whimper must have given him a clue how desperate she'd become. He dipped again, harder this time. "Come on. You want this cock up your ass. I know you do."

His words, nasty and exciting, fired her libido until she felt an orgasm hovering just out of reach.

He continued each extremely gentle plunge working deeper until she realized most of his cock possessed her ass. He initiated a steady thrust and retreat, never fucking too hard. Within seconds, the climax threatening to explode reached a height she couldn't contain. Her pussy rippled, clenching hard on the dildo while her anus tightened over his cock. A whimpering left her throat, then she moaned hard and long as climax shuddered through her being with an upwelling of hot bursts.

With a loud groan his completion erupted.

Panting, his body quivering in completion, he kissed her on the neck. He pulled out of her slowly, and she moaned as he left her body and removed the dildo.

"You okay?" he asked as he left the bed.

She smiled and turned over on her back. "I'm better than okay."

He left for the bathroom, then she took her turn washing up. She came back to his arms with a smile.

The night turned into fire, a blazing glory filled with desires and long-hidden revelations of body and soul. They explored things she never expected and anal sex with him she would do again.

"You've been wonderful," she said as he nestled her closer in his arms.

"So have you." His breath brushed her brow, and his arms tightened around her. "And I don't plan on letting you go for the rest of the night."

She couldn't find the right words, and tears surfaced.

He palmed her back, his warm, callused fingers and broad palm sliding with sensual awareness down to her ass.

He cupped her and held there. "Yes?"

She took a chance, wondering if she'd lost her mind. She moved out of his arms long enough to prop up on her forearm and look into his face. The single dim light threw a shaded glow over the strong planes of his cheekbones and the granite solidity of his jaw. A few days ago, she'd known him by name and sight, but understood little about him as a man. Tonight she knew a portion of his heart, and the sensuality, the sheer giving inside him melted her resistance.

Even the thought that she could become pregnant couldn't cool the way she felt about him.

Damn it, she was already more than half in love with him.

* * * * *

"Synna?" He smiled gently, waiting for her reply.

"I'm sorry, but I was just thinking."

A humorous tilt to his lips warned her that he wouldn't let her get away with that. "Sounds serious. Better not do too much or you'll get a headache."

She laughed. "For the head of a major intelligence agency, you have one hell of a sense of humor."

"Thank you. I'll take that as a compliment." He reached up and brushed hair away from her face. It flopped back into her eye. "Damn that didn't do much good."

"That's okay. Gives you an excuse to do it again."

A broad heart-gripping smile curved his mouth and her body melted in response. No man had a right to be so good-looking and so nice.

"I was going to say, I feel very safe and cared for with you. Now I'm afraid you're going to tell me not to get too comfortable."

Once more, he brushed the hair from her eyes. "You're worried that I'm in this for the sex and saving your life, then I'm going to say 'thanks for the good time, baby, but I've gotta go'?"

She nodded. "This all happened so fast. We barely know each other. I don't want you to think I'm a clinging vine. I-I'm not… My other relationships with men have been…" His gaze held understanding, so she plunged onward. "With two relationships in the past, I became too serious too quick."

"You fell fast."

"Yes."

"And they didn't feel the same."

"They acted like they did, for as long as it took to get the sex. Then they weren't interested anymore. I should have taken longer to know them. Maybe then I would have seen them for what they were."

Dark concentration filled the depths in his eyes. Seriousness drew his lips into a frown. "That they didn't know their heads from their asses. When I sleep with a woman it isn't a slam-bam-thank-you-ma'am situation."

He didn't sound insulted, but she worried a little. She cupped his jaw and savored the prickly, masculine evidence of his growing beard. "Then you're unusual. A lot of men can have casual sex without emotional attachment." She shrugged. "But I'm not saying anything new here."

A muscle jumped in his jaw and for a gut-wrenching second her old fears assaulted her. He would leave. He would walk out of her life and this would be it. All she would have would be memories.

Ian pushed his fingers through her hair, his touch exquisitely gentle. "I haven't had a ton of those meaningless sexual relationships you're talking about."

"Women must be coming on to you all the time."

"Why do you think that?"

"Because you're..." She worked to get the words passed her tight throat. "You're sexy as hell. You can't tell me women weren't turned on knowing you had a dangerous occupation in the military."

He nodded. "Alpha Unit had groupies."

"I thought so."

To her surprise, amusement brightened his eyes. "So it follows if there were groupies, that I took advantage of it?"

"Well..."

"Well nothing. Yeah, there were some attractive women and some wanted to go to bed with me. But I only took one of them up on it."

She sat up, her legs to the side, looking down on him.

He shifted until he also sat up and piled pillows behind his back. "About ten years ago, I fell in love with Maggie. She was an administrator at the Army post where I worked. And she wasn't a groupie. Her brother worked with me in Alpha Unit. She and I became intimate and things became thick and heavy fast. I thought I'd never love anyone but her ever again." His voice turned huskier, rough with emotion. He crossed his arms and the muscles bulged in his biceps. "One night I told her I loved her. I confessed something I'd never felt for a woman before, and she bolted away from me. Maggie said she couldn't get that serious about a man who put his life on the line so often."

Sharp recognition hit Synna. She understood him in that moment better than she'd understood anyone.

"She dumped you? You?"

A grin almost formed on his mouth, but then it failed. "Why is that a surprise?"

"Because you're gorgeous. You're intelligent, witty, gentle and a fantastic lover."

Her face heated as she realized everything she'd admitted.

A real smile crinkled around his eyes. "Thank you. You're doing my ego a lot of good here, you know?"

"You're also modest. How could a woman resist that?" she said a little sarcastically.

He wiggled his eyebrows, moved his arms to show off his biceps, and puffed out his already magnificent chest. "Any more compliments and my head might explode."

She wrinkled her nose. "I'm telling the truth. Any woman who doesn't think you're attractive is nuts."

With a low growl, he gathered her into his arms and pulled her down to him for a long, slow kiss. His lips devoured, his tongue staking a claim.

When he lifted his head, his gaze held curiosity, along with the beginnings of a new fire. "Do you trust my professional competence and that I know what I'm doing when it comes to SIA?"

The words came with full conviction and honesty straight from her heart. "I do."

"Then trust me with this night. I don't do one-night stands, and I don't play with a woman's heart. When I make love, I mean it."

Make love.

She knew a man rarely used those words over the more gritty descriptors unless they felt an emotional connection with a woman. A quiet stillness enveloped their cocoon. She wanted the happiness she felt and the caring she saw in his eyes to last forever.

"I should be able to take the moment and go with it, but it feels weighty," she said.

He nodded. "I want you safe. Making love to you to keep you safe is a sweet bonus. But if that wasn't the way to keep you alive and well, I'd still do whatever it took, Synna. We haven't known each other long, but it's how I feel about you."

He tilted her jaw up and pressed tender kisses to her neck. She closed her eyes, contentment flowing into her veins. A man had never been this honest with her in bed, and she wanted to believe his truthfulness one hundred percent.

His cock hardened against her leg, a bold, hot intruder. Pleasure coiled tight in her lower belly. She imagined the heat as he slid deep inside and started to thrust. A growing urge built, trembled, and dared her to reach for what she wanted now.

His hand slid down her hip, then his fingers searched between her legs. "Damn, you're hot and wet."

Husky and taut with tension, his words fired her libido. She arched her hips. Three of his fingers wedged deep, and she moaned. Each movement as he thrust his fingers deeper made her writhe in excitement.

A soft groan issued from his lips. One hard thigh parted her legs, then he lowered his hips between her thighs. She gasped as his hips plunged, forcing his cock through tight folds. She parted to welcome him, her flesh yearning for new rhythm, for the cadence that would bring them together in ecstatic dance.

Ian looked down on her flushed face, her half-open eyes, her parted, lush lips. Satisfaction pierced him. She wanted this joining, and it filled him with happiness and lust so powerful he thought he might explode with the first thrust. Nothing mattered but taking this woman, making her his until she never wanted another man inside her. He'd imprint his taste upon Synna, take her hard and fast and bring her to orgasm after orgasm. Plunging his naked cock into the heat between her thighs rocked his world. He'd never had unprotected sex before, but with her it felt sweet, hot, and mind-bending. He wanted it, craved it, must have it with her again and again.

She gripped his biceps and arched her hips. He hissed as sharp coils of desire rushed through his groin. She felt so silky, her pussy wrapped around his cock with a tight grip. Sizzling hot. Wet. Unbelievably sexy.

He had to fuck her hard. Now.

He drew back, then plowed into her tight channel. A yearning sound slipped from her throat. He pulled back, rammed hard and high. She went crazy. Whimpers left her throat, and she ground her hips upward into his, her muscles milking his flesh. Gritting his teeth, he struggled, almost losing control and spewing his load.

"Do it, do it," she said, her voice and eyes pleading with him. "Finish me."

He couldn't leave her hanging any longer, and his cock demanded movement, hungry for completion.

He nailed her.

Every collision of his hips against hers sent his screaming need higher. Her cries echoed in his ears as she moved against him. Turned on by her desperation, hanging on by a thin string, he powered into her. His body went into riot as scorching desire drove his hips into a grinding, churning motion.

Her groans came higher, hotter, louder.

He'd never felt anything so tight, so hot, so silky wet.

She came, her entire body shaking as one loud, definitive word left her lips. "Yes!"

With a roar he climaxed, his cock jerking and throbbing as he pushed as high inside her as he could go. Hot streams of cum shot from him as he convulsed.

Oh shit. Yes.

He sank into her arms and sighed deeply as his brain went fuzzy with tension release. He spent the night in her arms, exhaustion leading him into a deep sleep.

Chapter Nine

✇

There's something you must understand and see before the Halloween party.

Ian's written words still lingered in Synna's mind the next day as she ventured down in the elevator toward a part of SIA she never knew existed. When she'd awakened at five o'clock that morning and discovered he'd left without saying goodbye, she wondered if she'd made a huge mistake sleeping with him. They'd had spectacular sex three times last night. Three wonderful, risky encounters she would remember the rest of her life, no matter what happened from this day forward. Last night with Ian had blown her away, broken down barriers she never knew she had, released inhibitions and made her feel more alive than she had in years. Yes, the anal sex had been new and exciting, but more than that, she'd never encountered a more loving, warm appreciation from a man.

Yet unbidden worry this morning had sent her into the shower and dressed in record time. Downstairs she'd discovered a note, written on a piece of steno paper and scribbled in his action-oriented, bold handwriting.

Synna,

I'm sorry I had to leave early. I've got meetings part of the morning. At ten o'clock, I need to see you. There's something you must understand and see before the Halloween party. A special key card will be left in an envelope under your phone before seven o'clock. Keep it close and safe. Insert the key card into the L10 slot at the button of the keypad in the elevator. When you get to Level Ten you'll need to take two rights and then two lefts. Stop at the double doors labeled 888. Come in and I'll be there waiting for you.

Ian

Sure enough, the key awaited her under the phone on her desk.

She smiled as the elevator took its everlovin' sweet time reaching the mysterious Level Ten. The skullduggery amused her. Why the dramatics? Ian could have escorted her here.

Because he trusts me?

Perhaps. The thought sent stirrings of longing deep inside her. She couldn't forget his scent, and just thinking about him stirred anew her deepest longings.

Curiosity made her stomach tight with nervous energy as the elevator seemed to take forever. The elevator pinged, and she jerked out of her reverie. She held her breath as the doors slid open. She stepped into the sterile hallway, and the off-white walls and dimmer lighting surprised her. Then again, what had she expected? Fluorescent lights and stark dreariness? Here the muted hallway boasted a few modernistic paintings that didn't suit her tastes. She withdrew the notepaper from her pocket and studied directions he'd give her. She'd heard rumors it was possible to get lost in the massive subbasement.

To her relief, she found the way easier than she anticipated. Double doors and the number 888 showed she'd made it. She knocked hard and the door popped open.

Ian stood in the doorway. All the breath left her lungs for a startled second. She'd had sex with him, reached heights she didn't know her body could reach. She expected his primal masculinity to have less influence on her mind and body.

No getting around facts. He is sexy as hell.

"Come on in," he said without preamble, his gaze coasting over her in an almost impersonal inspection she found somehow disappointing.

She stepped inside, her wide-legged pants swishing around her mid-heel pumps. She tucked the instructions back in her pocket. As she stepped into the large room, she felt swallowed by the gigantic conference room that was not unlike several upstairs. This room, though, owned more amenities. A large, expensive-looking leather couch sat against one wall, and a corpulent matching chair dwarfed the corner next to it. A coffee table, end tables and antique-style lamps on a low setting completed the picture. In contrast to the hall outside, this room held a comfortable, almost homey ambiance along with the business aspects. A mahogany-colored desk dominated the other end of the room. Scattered photographs from past years at the SIA framed the walls.

The conference room would be a perfect for a midmorning rendezvous. Ian's grin was wide and determined, as if he knew exactly what she thought.

"Cozy," she said as he closed and locked the door behind her.

The snick of the lock sounded so final.

"This is where we usually have our Level Ten meetings."

She lifted one eyebrow. "I'm impressed. But why am I here in secret squirrel land, Ian?"

He smiled again and warmth stole through her. God, did he have to look so damned gorgeous? So tough, strong, and vulnerable all at once? The heavens gave this man everything necessary to drive a woman crazy on more than one occasion. What had she done to deserve the agony and ecstasy of knowing him?

He took a step closer and it brought his tantalizing male scent nearer as well. She drew in a deep breath.

His gaze enveloped her until she couldn't see anything, feel anything but him. His body conveyed infinite strength combined with determination to protect.

"Two reasons why you're here." He reached out and brushed her cheek with the back of his fingers. Sparks of arousal filtered into her body and she shivered with deep longing for more. "Do you regret what we did last night? Do you want out of the mission?"

A little flabbergasted, she gazed at him openmouthed. With a heaving breath, she found her voice. "No to both questions. I thought we were settled, at least, on the mission." When he didn't speak, a series of depressing thoughts poured into her mind like a flood. "Wait. Are you saying you regretted last night and that you want me off the mission?"

He shook his head. "If we don't put Tyler back in the Shadow Realm, he'll continue coming after you. You'll need protection. Even if it means putting you under twenty-four guard. Forever."

She gave a half-mocking laugh, thinking of such constraint incomprehensible. "I couldn't live like that. I'd die. Anyone would die."

He shook his head. "No. There are people who've lived under guard most of their lives, whether they wanted it or not." His eyes saddened. "That's one reason why we have to take this weredemon thing to its conclusion. Anything else would be intolerable."

"I couldn't take that. I'd shrivel."

"I know. That's why we have to see this through."

"S-see it through. It sounds so impersonal." She didn't know how to express the thoughts running around in her mind. Everything seemed as mixed as vegetable soup, as murky as a deep ocean. She must ask the question if she wanted the truth. "Do you wish we hadn't...you know?"

One of his brows went up, his mouth quirking in a quick, sexy tilt she found irresistible. He slipped his hand behind her neck and into her hair. His embracing heat sent shivers of desire tingling all the way down her spine to settle deep in her lower stomach.

"I can't stop thinking about last night. The way we were together. How hot you were, your skin, your tongue," he said huskily.

Her heart picked up the beat as his hot breath touched her forehead. He pressed a kiss there. As his chest brushed her breasts, her nipples prickled and tightened. She reached up and touched his chest, her fingers smoothing along the warmth of his blue sweater, digging into his heat with a soft moan.

"I'm never going to forget what we did last night. Are you?" he asked.

She could hide behind modesty, pretend nothing happened beyond a pleasant interlude. "How could I disregard the most toe-curling, erotic evening of my life?"

His mouth touched her temple again, then trailed down until he whispered in her ear, the deep, husky resonance sending heat waves along her body. "Oh, man."

His body shivered against hers, the indication that he felt as turned on as she did sent her confidence and need into the heavens. "Does that mean last night was special for you?"

Ian kissed her ear, then his lips pinpointed the tender skin just below. "I'm having a helluva time keeping my mind on business. You've rocked my world, Synna. I can't stop wanting to touch you." He punctuated each statement with a kiss, then another, until he worked his way to her lips. "I can't stop wanting this."

His mouth enveloped hers in a hot, drugging kiss that melted resistance. His tongue took instant possession. Each deep plunge, each stroke of his tongue over hers brought desire higher within her. She responded with unrestrained passion, her heart beating a frantic, needy rhythm and demanding more from her depths. She couldn't release the high-stakes hunger building inside as his body moved against hers in sensual counterpoint. Hard, masculine angles cradled and sheltered her softness, and she'd never felt more feminine than at this moment. His hands cupped her butt and squeezed, then palmed upward over her back, searching hollows and curves. He fondled her with eagerness, and she knew his restraint hung by a tiny thread. Inflamed, she gripped his shoulders and savored his body against hers.

Then she remembered where they were, and she broke away, pushing at his chest. "No. We can't. Not here."

He moaned softly, and his kisses trailed over her face to her ear where he whispered, "I want you so much."

She felt his control teetering, and she wasn't far behind. One more hot, tongue-thrusting kiss, one more touch of his hard cock against her and they'd combust. He moaned and tasted her neck, his tongue tracing an erotic path over her skin.

"Ian. We have to stop."

Breathing hard, he took a step back. His gaze glittered with a hard intensity that would have frightened her if she didn't understand already that it came from desire. "There aren't any cameras in here and the room is off-limits for an hour. But you're right. That's not what I asked you to come here for. I wanted to show you something."

He walked toward a tall, dark metal cabinet on one side of the room and slid open the doors to reveal ten gleaming metal swords. Each sword featured red satin cording attached to the hilt so they hung in place inside the red interior. Their hilts were a strange kaleidoscope of colors, almost like the pearlescent glow of an abalone shell. They looked lethal as hell, a slightly shorter version of a broadsword.

She stepped forward as curiosity pushed her. "What are these?"

He lifted one out of the cabinet and handed it to her. "Electrical converter swords. They're new at SIA. A prototype for a standard weapon that will be in every agent's arsenal soon. How does that feel in your hands?"

She hefted the object by the hilt, feeling the extraordinary featherlight material. "It's incredible. What does it do other than stab people?"

He grinned. "I'd give a demonstration, but this isn't the place to do it. What I wanted you to do is know how to use one. I'll have one at the Halloween party, and so will Ben Darrock."

Her eyes widened as she placed the cold metal on the conference table. "Are you saying I'm going to carry one of these around?"

"No, no. But I wanted you to know how to use it." He picked up the weapon and handed it to her again. "Here, hold it."

He came around behind her, his arms slipping about her waist and snuggling her against his body. She wanted to moan with ecstasy as his big body wrapped her in security and heat. He felt so hot, so strong, and the sensations darting through her body made her almost dizzy. His hips pressed against her backside, and his erection hardened against her.

His hands clamped firmly over hers, holding the sword grip tightly within their combined grasp. "Feel that. Now close your eyes." A little reluctant, she glanced back at him. "Come on, honey. I need you to do this for me. It's important."

Honey. Glimmers of quicksilver arousal touched her stomach and went straight down to her loins. Possessive and protective, his embrace fired every feminine fiber into life.

"If things go to hell," he said softly against her temple, "I want you to protect yourself."

"But if I'm not carrying it with me—"

"If anything happens to me while we're together at the party you'll know how to pick up my weapon and use it."

She stiffened in his arms, the thought of him hurt or dead spearing her heart like a knife. "No. Nothing is going to happen to you."

"You don't know that."

Her grip tightened on the hilt, but she said nothing.

He let a few seconds pass, then continued. His fingers tightened over hers. "Here, draw it up like this. See this button near the thumb? It's a safety switch. You press it first, then if you hit the red switch on the jeweled hilt a huge stream of light spills out of the tip like a laser."

Amazed, she moved her fingers under his. "Who thinks up these things?"

"There are several employees charged with designing weapons. People like Dorky."

"Dorky?"

"Yeah. She's on the research team."

"I take it this sword is used for k-killing…otherworldly dangers."

He kissed her ear and her eyes about rolled back in her head with pleasure. "You got it."

"Is the edge sharp, too?"

"Yep. Sharp enough to cut off a demon head or slice paper."

"God. All this power under my fingertips. Kind of heady."

He chuckled, and the vibration went through her back and straight to her heart. In that moment she felt a warming, an indescribably beautiful desire to bond with him always. To give him whatever he needed, support, love, her body and soul.

"Let's put this down," he said, moving their combined grip until the sword slipped onto the conference table, "before I lose control and do something dangerous."

"Such as?" she asked breathlessly.

"Such as try and kiss you while we're still gripping this sword. Not a good idea."

Ian wrapped his arms around her middle and brought her closer against him once more, and she leaned her head back so it rested on his shoulder. She offered her neck and he brushed her hair away so he could kiss her. His palms traced up over her breasts. He plucked her nipples softly, and she shivered in spine-melting ecstasy. She'd worn a thin scrap of a bra that supported but allowed her nipples to show if she became cold or aroused.

He tongued her ear and said, "If you don't want this now, tell me."

She did want it. Her pussy ached, her breathing quickened, and her heart took up the pace. As he rubbed over her nipples, she shivered and couldn't hold back a gentle moan. She'd go insane. The man knew how to turn her on faster than a pilot light. Heat flared as his touch slipped down to cup her mound for a quick, tantalizing second.

"Ian," she gasped.

"Yes?" His breath came hot against her cheek as he kissed her there.

"What are we doing?"

"Mmmm." He didn't really answer, his hands traveling a more explicit path as he again encompassed her breasts and plucked her nipples. "These sweet little nipples are sticking up through your blouse. Damn, honey." His next curse came low and without restraint. "Shit, you have beautiful nipples. Has anyone ever told you that?"

"No."

His hands came up and worked open the buttons on her blouse. She quivered as he found the front hook and flicked it open with one movement of his hands. As he enveloped her naked breasts in his hot palms, her pussy clenched. She felt moisture trickle and dampen her panties.

"Oh God, Ian."

He tweaked her nipples quickly and the sharp little tug made her almost scream for relief.

"Tell me this isn't a good idea," he said, his voice rough with desire.

"It isn't a good idea."

"We should stop."

"We should."

"Are we?" His tongue dipped into her ear and swirled.

She shivered and moaned. "No. Please. We can't stop now."

His hands went to the waistband on her pants and quickly undid the button and zipper. His fingers plunged into her panties and smoothed down her stomach to her pubic hair. "Should I touch you?"

"Please." She didn't care if she begged.

His fingers bypassed her clit and went right for the soaked folds. As he plied her hot, weeping flesh, she whimpered.

"Shit," he whispered. "God, you drive me insane. You're so wet."

Such ability to drive a man to the edge made her ego swell with feminine energy. "I'm not trying to drive you nuts."

"I know, but I...I should keep my hands off you. I—"

"Don't." She eased his hand out of her pants, then turned around in his embrace and captured his face between her hands. "Don't stop feeling this way. I know I can't."

She threw away her last caution. She tugged his head down and kissed him, softly at first. He allowed her to caress his lips tenderly. Then she tasted Ian with eager abandon. She wanted him out of control, ready to do anything and everything. As she pushed one hand into his thick hair, she licked his lower lip. With a soft growl, he thrust his tongue inside her mouth. As he anchored her against his body, his hands searched her secrets. Repeatedly he plundered her mouth, took her senses on a whirlwind tour of pulse-pounding ecstasy.

She wanted him more than breath, more than life, and she would have him. Nothing could stop her from tasting, touching, making love to him. His cock pushed against her, already hard and ready. She moved her hips, and his breath hissed inward as his arms tightened around her waist. His fingers speared into her hair and tugged her head back so he could reach her throat. He worked upon her desires, licking, kissing the column until she quaked. Dazzled by her ability to turn him on, and the strength of her longings, she moved against him in sinuous, indolent desire. She wanted him with a furious, urgent heat. Sensations melted together in a volcanic rush with no beginning or end, piling one upon the other in a race to find the ultimate feeling. His cock grew bigger, longer and she reached for it. Her fingers curved around him and measured his length with long strokes up and down.

He jerked and then groaned into her mouth. "Son of a bitch."

She laughed, drunk on her influence over his response. "Is that good or bad?"

"Good." He kissed her again as he pressed her hand against his cock. "So good."

She broke away to whisper against his lips, "I want you."

He grinned, his eyes hot with adore and amusement. "Then have me."

Unrestrained, she hurried to unbuckle his belt. When she wrestled open his pants, and freed his cock, she almost went down on him. Before she could move, he leaned down and pulled off her shoes, then yanked off her pants and panties. She giggled, the silly sound embarrassing her. A feral, heated response ignited in his eyes. He looked everything that he was. Dangerous, strong, and turned on.

He lifted her up and placed her on the edge of the conference table. He leaned over and latched onto one nipple, his tongue and lips sucking hard and fast. She writhed in his hold, so excited she couldn't keep the whimpers back.

Ian drew back, his breathing heavier, his eyes molten with need. He eyed her pussy. "Lean back."

Excited, she lay back on the table and bent her knees so her femininity lay fully exposed to his gaze and touch. Then without further preliminaries, he bent his knees, aligned his cock with her pussy, and plunged. She groaned as his long, broad length stretched, then retreated, then thrust again. He didn't stay still, he continued the motion, his need and hers mingling in a wild fight to the finish.

His eyes held an animal intensity she found thrilling and arousing. She clasped her thighs and opened her legs wider.

"Yeah. That's it," he rasped.

She closed her eyes and allowed his untamed wishes to sweep her away. Sharp, hungry thrusts pierced her pussy as he pounded deep. His thrusts quickened and she felt orgasm coming faster than she would have imagined. Each time his cock thrust, it rubbed insistently over her G-spot, the pull and push stimulating nerve endings deep inside. She panted with excitement and moved her hips to his beat. His hands slipped under her ass as he powered into her.

His hips churned against hers with hot, banging thrusts that sent her excitement higher and higher. She'd never felt anything this intense before, and her heart pounded so hard she could hardly find her breath. Physical sensations rushed forward and swamped tender feelings. No time for affectionate words under the onslaught of unbridled lust.

A swift burn built high in her pussy. Without mercy, it burst like a supernova. Her hips jerked against his as she squirmed. She writhed and skewered herself on the hot, hard cock burrowing into her relentlessly. As her pussy contracted over his cock, she barely stifled a shriek. Her cry of ecstasy came out as an uninhibited groan that rumbled from deep inside. Her entire body quaked as her orgasm rolled in a gigantic wave. Muscles clenched, breathing ceased, and for a moment, she knew the heady ecstasy of the heavens.

With a last lunge, he jammed his cock deep and released with a shout. She watched his eyes snap shut, his lips draw back in a grimace as he quivered, shook and panted. It turned her on even more, and her pussy tightened again, wanting another orgasm with a greedy search for fulfillment. She tilted her hips upward, and his cock caressed her inside.

"Holy shit," he said between gasps for breath.

As if he could read her mind, he reached down, clasped her clit between finger and thumb, and tugged with a steady rhythm. She shivered with excitement, a soft moan parting her lips. "Yes."

He kept his cock deep and hard inside her while he plucked and strummed the tender flesh that throbbed and ached for another completion. "Come on, honey. Take it all."

She closed her eyes and arched into his hand, grabbed onto the sensation as he took her higher, higher, and higher yet. Heaven waited and held. Another single sharp tug on her clit did the trick. Orgasm burst and heat flooded her pussy as she gasped and moaned and shamelessly took him with greedy abandon. When she settled down to earth, he withdrew and she opened her eyes.

"I can't believe we just did that," she said with a smile.

His smile became warm and wicked. He reached for a box of tissues sitting on the table and they used them to clean up. "I'm damn glad we did."

After they'd rearranged their clothing, she noticed the scent of sex in the air. "Uh…anyone who comes is g-going to know what we were doing in here."

He shook his head and drew her into his arms. "No. The air recirculates in this place quickly."

She sighed. "Good."

He kissed her forehead and titled her chin up so she looked deep into his eyes. "We'd better get back to work, though."

"All right." She smiled a little self-consciously, then started toward the door.

He reached for her arm and tugged her back for another deep, sweet kiss. Warmth and tenderness burned in his gaze as he released her. She cupped his face and savored touching him so intimately.

"If you need me, don't hesitate to call," he said.

She left the conference room with a glow around her heart, and the knowledge that whatever happened, Ian felt more than overwhelming passion for her. He really cared.

Chapter Ten

೪೨

Synna took her time traveling back from a meeting to her cubicle that afternoon. As she walked, she daydreamed shamelessly about her encounter earlier that morning with Ian. She'd never imagined that less than a week ago, she'd be Ian Frasier's lover. Such good fortune seemed impossible. Her happiness reached new heights as she recalled his tenderness and willingness to share his thoughts and feelings. Maybe, just maybe, she could trust him with everything about herself.

The idea terrified her in a brand-new way. Most men didn't want that much information about a woman. They could have sex with a woman, but not intend to get to know her deepest secrets. Ian didn't seem like that kind of man. He'd given so much of himself since they'd become lovers. She would take it slow, and make sure her heart stayed guarded enough to prevent complete destruction if he changed his mind about her. Ian hadn't called her this afternoon, but then she hadn't expected him to. She reminded herself for the third time that just because they were lovers didn't mean they didn't have jobs to do and other obligations.

She stopped daydreaming right as a shadow appeared out of a dark office doorway and latched onto her arm.

"What—?"

Her throat tightened on a gasp as an arm swept around her waist and tugged her into the office. She could barely see, but she knew with absolute certainty, the arm around her waist didn't belong to Ian. The door closed, then the overhead light came on.

Tyler.

"Tyler, what is going on?" She kept her voice steady and tried keep alarm out of her voice. Her stomach tumbled with anxiety, and she could feel all the hairs on her body prickling as she tensed for an attack.

Ian had warned her about being alone with Tyler. What could she do if he did jump her? Scream bloody murder?

Tyler stood with his back to the door, his face flushed, his breathing a little heavy. He put one hand up before she could speak. "Don't panic."

Her heart pounded, her mouth dry. "What the hell are you doing? You scared the crap out of me."

A hunted light entered his eyes. "I'm sorry I grabbed you, but I needed to speak with you again before the Halloween party."

Impatient, she hoped this little scene was nothing more than Tyler's weird demon humor. She crossed her arms. "You couldn't just call me or stop by the cubicle?"

"I didn't want Heidi seeing me with you."

Curiosity overcame unease. "Why do you care if anyone sees you with me? Especially Heidi."

"Because she's—look, I can't tell you everything. But I don't mean you any harm, you've got to believe that. No matter what happens at the Halloween party, I don't mean you any harm."

She believed that as much as hearing scientists say they'd changed their minds and that the moon really was made of cheese. Blue cheese, in fact. "What's going to happen at the party?"

He stiffened, as if someone poked him from behind, his lanky body tensed and on edge. Like a gazelle, he might leap at any moment. "I don't know for sure, but it's important you stay near me. It's the only way I can protect you." He puffed up his scrawny chest and placed his hands on his hips. "Don't worry. I've got you covered. I'm buff."

Buff? Next to Ian, the weredemon rated a one on the brawn scale. A two if he was lucky. Ian would pulverize Tyler.

He stepped forward, and she took a step back. "Come on, Synna. You need me to protect you."

She couldn't help it. A huge guffaw snorted from her gut in a very unladylike manner. The laugh built into a roar, until she held her stomach and bent over.

"What the hell is so funny?" he asked with an indignant growl. "I'm trying to be serious here."

Another even more hysterical cackle ripped up from her belly.

Her mind screamed for control. *Get a grip any time now, Synna.*

She managed, between gasps, to sneak in a few words. "I-I'm sorry. It-It's just that I—you—"

"Thanks a lot." His voice sounded petulant rather than angry. "I can't believe you're laughing at me. You think I can't protect you?"

She immediately felt bad, even though she shouldn't. The man was a damned demon, for God's sake. Why should she feel bad about hurting his feelings? Still, the skullduggery had inched up to the ridiculous stage. "I'm sorry. I really am. It's just that I've been under a lot of pressure to get Heidi up to speed before I leave the SIA. I'm on edge. Then you come along and said I was in danger and it sounded preposterous."

He glared, and she could see he didn't believe her. Oh, hell. She couldn't tell him that she'd chortled because she didn't think he could defend her. With demon powers, perhaps he could.

"You're in more danger than you can imagine," he said.

Sorrow replaced his indignation, and his eyes looked almost misty with tears.

If she didn't know about his demon status, she'd almost feel like mothering him. Maybe if he'd give up valuable information, she could save him from the worst punishment SIA had to offer. "What kind of danger?"

He jammed his hands in his pockets. "I can't tell you specifics."

She put her hands on her hips. "So I'm just supposed to take your word for it. I'm in some mysterious danger."

"Right."

"Why? I mean, why should I believe you? What motivation do I have?"

"Because I'm—because I know things about this world that you don't. About things that could harm you. Take my word for it."

She shook her head. "Tyler, I don't need your help or your protection. Let's take this slowly, okay. We have a date for the party and we can get to know each other better then."

Before she could take another breath, the door burst open and Tyler lurched forward toward her. He reached out and yanked her into his arms.

Ian stood alone in the doorway, his gaze hard and harsh. "Let her go. Now."

Stunned by his appearance, she stayed in Tyler's embrace. Tyler didn't say a word and when she glanced up at him he looked equally shell-shocked.

Ian stepped inside. His hands balled into fists at his sides, a thunderous glare in his eyes. Rough and husky, his voice came clear again. "I said, let her go."

She squirmed in Tyler's arms. Oh God. What if Ian thought she'd met up with Tyler alone on purpose? He might think—oh, jeez.

Horrified, she did another twist and wrested out of Tyler's arms. "This isn't what it looks like."

Ian's expression didn't change. He still looked pissed. "I need to speak with her alone, Hessler."

Tyler's eyes hardened with resentment. "Why?"

"It's none of your damned business," Ian said.

Tyler glared. "Right. I see how it is. You want her for yourself."

Ian didn't say anything, matching Tyler's glare.

Tyler tossed one last resentful glance at them both. "Well, she's going to the party with me. That says something."

Tyler left the room and slammed the door. Ian locked the door, then stalked toward her. This time she didn't back away from his anger.

Before she could speak, he enveloped her in his arms and tucked her close. "Are you all right? Did he hurt you? Please tell me he didn't kiss you."

"No, he didn't kiss me. I'm fine."

His solid arms held her tight. His fingers plunged into the hair at the back of her head and pressed her cheek against his shoulder. Stiff with surprise, she waited for him to speak.

When he didn't, she broke down and spoke first. "Ian, what's wrong?"

"What's wrong?" His voice was hoarse with emotion. He drew back to look deep into her eyes, but kept her within his embrace. "You were alone with that bastard. I *told* you never to be alone with him. Are you trying to get hurt or killed?"

"No, no. He dragged me in here. I was just walking down the hall when this door opened and suddenly I'm dragged into this barely bigger than a closet…" She looked around. "Well, it *is* a closet. A very large but empty storage closet."

His eyes went supernova with anger. "What the hell did he want?"

"He said he wanted to protect me at the Halloween party." She went on to explain everything Tyler had said. "I laughed at him."

Ian's eyes widened. "You laughed? Why?"

"The idea of scrawny Tyler wanting to protect me seemed ludicrous. With everything that has happened lately, it just hit my funny bone wrong. I went hysterical."

"What did he do?"

She couldn't help but smile. "Actually, not much. I could tell I hurt his feelings. Do you think maybe he's telling the truth about that part? About something bad happening at the party and that he wants to keep me safe?"

Ian didn't look convinced as he slowly eased her out of his arms. "I think it means he's playing with you."

"Why bother?"

He shrugged. "Because it's what weredemons do well. They play with a human's emotions. You can't let your guard down for a moment."

Within the deep emotions in his eyes, she saw genuine caring and concern, a man worried about her on a visceral level. It drove her to reach up and pull his head down for a quick, soft kiss. She released him and glanced around. "If anyone sees us coming out of here—"

"I know." He smiled wanly. "They'll think we were making out. Do you care what anyone thinks?"

She hesitated, then drew a deep breath and went with her solid intuition. "Only if it damages your reputation and makes life difficult."

He shook his head and traced her cheek with his index finger. Heat stirred in her loins. "Don't worry about me. Just concentrate on staying safe until the party. If there is additional danger, we'll handle it."

"How did you know I was in this closet?"

"I wouldn't have known, but Dorky saw you on one of the camera monitors and also saw Tyler snatch you." He shook his head. "When she alerted me, I almost came unglued. I thought…" He shook his head again. "I ran down here. Then, seeing you in his arms made me crazy. If he had done anything to you, I would have broken him in two."

She smiled. "You looked angry, all right. I thought you might hit him."

"Believe me, I was tempted." He heaved a deep breath.

She reached up and brushed her fingers over his chest. "Thank you."

"For what?"

"Watching out for me."

He leaned closer, his eyes slumberous with desire. "Always."

Her breath caught, and he sealed his mouth to hers for a gentle taste.

She pulled back. "I'd better get back to work."

Ian winked and his voice went low and husky. "You'd better. A few more minutes in here, and I'd be fucking you up against that wall."

She flushed. *God, that sounds delicious.*

"Ian."

His slow, sensual smile sent wicked, stirring desire straight to her core. "Go now. I'm having a hard enough time keeping my hands off you. I'll see you tonight at the party."

She forced herself to leave him and the major testosterone that ran off him in buckets. As she walked down the corridor, she half expected to see Tyler materialize. She made it to her cubicle and settled into her chair to peruse how she could make it through the next few hours.

Chapter Eleven

๛

Ian paced the length of the party more than once, his patience stretching thin. Already the crowd numbered in the hundreds.

"I've heard rumors there's a crazy man wanderin' the party." A tall man about his height wearing a black Stetson walked up to Ian. He wore a red western shirt, bolo tie, leather vest, jeans and brown cowboy boots. Division Six Director Ben Darrock's Scottish accent was at odds with his costume. The first time he met the Director, he'd found deep respect for the man and the way he ran his department. He had things in common with Ben, and they'd gotten along well from the start. Ben wasn't intimidated by the fact Ian was head of SIA, and Ian respected the other man's strength.

He handed a paper cup of punch to Ian. "Somethin' wrong?"

Keeping his voice low, Ian almost growled the words, "Damn right something is wrong. Synna isn't here yet."

Ben took a sip of punch from his own cup. "It's barely seven. Some people like to be fashionably late." He grinned irreverently. "You're about to wear a hole in the floor."

Ian grunted and stared at the small paper cup swallowed up by his hand. "This better be alcohol-free. I need to be alert for trouble."

"It's virgin punch. And stop worryin'." Ben's accent went a little thicker. "You'll send out so many vibes that when Tyler arrives, he'll notice somethin' wrong. You're frothin' at the mouth."

The thought of Synna alone with a weredemon tore at Ian's guts. Having sex with her had made his smoldering feelings for her grow even deeper. Not only did he want to slide into her warm, wet body again, when he got his hands on her tonight—

How do I feel?

Shit. His emotions jumped from one extreme to another. One moment he wanted to yank her into a back room, rip off her panties and fuck her hard and fast, the next he wanted to build up the tension and wait. Lastly, he knew he cared more about her than any woman he'd known.

It scared the hell out of him.

"This isn't right," Ian said. "We shouldn't have allowed Synna to do this."

"She said she would, remember?"

"She was ordered to."

Ben nodded. "I understand you're worried."

Ian's gaze snapped to Ben's. "Is it that obvious?"

Ben's irreverent grin confirmed the worst. "Anyone paying close attention has to know that you've got feelings for Synna."

With a groan, Ian said, "At this point, I don't care if the SIA wants to fire me. Synna is more important."

He drew this knowledge deep into his bones like a man drowning. His top priority, right now and in the future, was Synna MacDell. All other considerations, including his position as head of SIA, would have to take a back seat if danger came anywhere near her.

Ian didn't think anything would help this grinding foreboding until this ball-busting assignment finished and Synna lay safe in his arms. He gulped down the punch and put the empty cup on a table. "They should be here any minute."

Ben's glance landed on the sword. "You plannin' on using that if the time comes?"

Ian encircled the sword grip and tightened his fingers. "You're damned right. It'll come in handy."

Ben pushed the brim of his hat higher up and peered at Ian. "It'll make a mess."

Ian grinned. "Exactly."

* * * * *

Tyler's hand pressed the small of Synna's back as he guided her into the foyer of Adora Hall, the huge room SIA used for a party facility. On the grounds of the secure SIA complex, the large Grecian-looking building boosted many columns along the front façade, as well as a palatial back area replete with gardens, a pool, and a few guest suites set up for visiting dignitaries.

Bombarded by noise from the crowded foyer, Synna now wished she'd worn something less revealing than the wench costume. Under the long, black wool coat, she felt vulnerable. As she stood in the two-story foyer with Tyler touching her back, she wanted to run far away where neither the SIA nor weredemons could find her.

"This is awesome," Tyler said, his eyes a little wide, his mouth open in surprise.

"You've never been here?"

"Never." As she started to slide off her coat, he asked, "What about you? How would you like to give me a tour?"

She remembered Ian's admonition not to let Tyler get her alone.

As he took her coat and handed it to the coat check woman, Synna looped her small black velvet handbag over her shoulder. "Why don't we go in and chat with a few people first?"

Tyler shrugged, his shoulders looking broader in the pirate costume. When he'd picked her up in his small white sedan, she half expected him to wear the same nerdy attire he usually did. Even if Tyler wasn't a weredemon and didn't have a sinister agenda, she still wouldn't find him attractive. Ian had put his stamp on her, his mark, and she'd never be the same. Another man could kiss her, caress her, make love to her, and it wouldn't matter. Ian had imprinted himself on her soul forever.

They wandered into the main room. Three glittering crystal chandeliers dominated the high ceiling, as well as moldings and frescos. Large tapestries depicting Greek and Roman escapades graced four walls. Topiaries hugged the corners, and long, red velvet curtains draped large multi-paned windows. Laughter and the scent of warm appetizers teased her nose. Tables decorated with black tablecloths groaned under the weight of food, as well as orange nonalcoholic punch and sparkling champagne. Employees wearing every imaginable costume boogied on the dance floor to the song "Monster Mash". Most people wore sinister costumes, but the occasional pink bunny gave the party a less serious aspect.

Synna eyed the paper bats, ghosts and pumpkins strung everywhere. All in all, a festive situation.

She would love to treat the party as nothing more than a good time. In the back of her mind lingered the danger.

"Champagne?" Tyler asked Synna as a woman walked by with a tray.

"Sure." She snatched a tall flute of bubbly at the same he did, and took a hearty sip.

Heidi, wearing a gypsy costume, fluttered toward them with a grin. "Hey, guys. Isn't this great?" She patted Tyler on the shoulder. "You look wonderful. Tyler, what are you supposed to be?"

Tyler must have caught the slight sarcasm in Heidi's tone. He smirked. "A pirate. You couldn't tell?"

Heidi grinned. "Better than the devil in dinner wear. What am I?"

"Obviously you're a gypsy," Synna said.

"Not just any gypsy. A fortune teller."

"Uh-huh." Tyler slammed down the remainder of his champagne and gave it to a passing server. "What can you tell me about my future?"

"That'll cost you ten dollars." Heidi produced an envelope from a pocket in the voluminous skirt she wore. She explained which local charities the money would benefit.

"I'll do it." Synna stepped forward, fidgeting in her purse for money.

Heidi snatched two fives from Synna's hand. "This way. I have a table at the other end."

Tyler started to follow, but Heidi put a hand on his chest. "Readings are personal. Wait your turn."

He smirked. "Okay. Whatever you say." He turned away and followed a woman carrying a platter of appetizers.

As Heidi led the way through the crowd, they stopped several times to say hello to co-workers. Synna scanned the throng, but she didn't see a sign of Ian. Butterflies did barrel rolls in her stomach. He'd refused to say what he planned to wear. He explained that he wanted her reaction clear and uninhibited. She'd almost asked him if was wearing a loincloth. The weather had turned extraordinary cold, but she wouldn't have been surprised if he came to the party half-naked to drive her nuts.

Oh yes. It would drive her batty all right. Anticipation made her heart thunder, and fear made her wonder if she could pull off this sham. She'd paid the ten dollars to get away from Tyler for a few moments, as well as for the good cause. She'd started to feel so strange around him, as if he might at some point read her mind and know what the SIA planned for his sorry demon ass.

The music turned from rock to a symphony of monsters, wolves, bat shrieks and unearthly screams.

"Here we are." Heidi stopped by a table draped in purple satin gauze and violent red braiding. Shocking to the eyes, but appropriate for Heidi's ambiance. "Have a seat."

Feeling a little foolish, Synna settled into one of the two metal folding chairs.

"You seem glad to leave Tyler." Heidi sat in the other chair and put her hands on the lid of a dark wood box. A deeply carved ankh graced the beautiful wood. "I can't say I blame you."

Synna refused to get into a conversation about her predicament. "Everything is fine."

Heidi nodded, the turban around her forehead bobbing. "Ian will be glad to hear it."

Surprise made Synna blink. She stared at the gypsy across the table. "What?"

"I'm your safety contact. Ian and Quinton put me on this detail just this morning and asked me to check on you. How are things going with Tyler?"

Startled, Synna nodded. "I'm fine. Everything is running like clockwork right now." Synna frowned. "Ian didn't say anything about putting you on this detail when I talked with him this morning."

Heidi shrugged. "He probably did it right after he talked to you. Or maybe he just forgot to tell you."

Heidi spread Egyptian tarot cards out on the table. The beautifully colored cards depicted hieroglyphics, and monuments such as The Sphinx, and The Great Pyramids of Giza.

"These cards," Heidi said with a dramatic tone, "will tell you the key to your future."

Uninterested in the theatrics, Synna kept her voice low as she asked, "What do you know about Tyler?"

Heidi lowered her voice. "Just what Ian told me this morning. Now, how are you really?" Heidi put one last card down. "Are you holding up?"

"I'm good." Then it occurred to her that Ian may not even be at the party yet. Had he decided to let other people handle the situation? "Where is Ian?"

Heidi's lips curved into a devilish smile. "Patience."

Heidi's gaze clouded for a second as she looked at the spread of cards.

"Don't I have to ask you a question?" Synna asked.

"Yep. Go for it."

Synna pondered, uncertain.

"Don't think about it too long. What's the burning question in your mind right now?"

Synna let out with it. "Will tonight turn out all right?"

Heidi surveyed the cards. She pointed to a card showing The Temple at Karnak. A frown replaced her earlier cheerful attitude.

Heidi glanced up, her eyes clouded with uncertainty. "This is pretty interesting. A little hard to read. I'm usually good at this but…" She scanned the cards again. "This indicates you aren't ready for what is to come. Almost everything you see tonight will have more than one side. This means you will experience confusion. There is something being hidden from you."

Synna grinned, unable to take the information seriously. "How long have you been reading these cards as a hobby?"

Heidi drew back a little, no longer gazing at the configuration in front of her. "Honey, I've been reading them since I was twelve. My great-grandmother was a voodoo priestess and a friend of Marie Laveux."

"Marie Laveux of New Orleans? The Queen of Voodoo?"

"Yes." Heidi fiddled with a scarf at her neck, as if it irritated her. Or, maybe the way Synna dismissed the cards angered Heidi. "They were great friends. This deck has been in my family and passed down from generation to generation."

"They're beautiful cards."

Heidi didn't look pacified. "Now, the Sphinx card symbolizes leaving the past behind and start a brand-new track." A broad smile broke over her round face. "Now this one is really nice. You will find a new lover or you have found one already."

Synna wasn't surprised at Heidi's accuracy about leaving the past. She knew Synna was leaving the agency. As for the new lover, well…

Music spilled out of the speakers, a sultry, smooth jazz tune that insinuated sinful pleasures all wrapped in body chocolate with a strawberry in the navel. Synna ignored it.

"This card, the Phoenix, suggests you're rising from the ashes of everything before in your life that hasn't worked for you." Heidi nodded, satisfaction in her smile. "Your heart will benefit, your health. Your soul." Heidi touched the Mummy card with her index finger and frowned. "This card, in this configuration, is unpleasant. It's an…"

"Yes?"

"An omen of danger."

A dark cloud passed over Synna's thoughts, and her intuition told her that Heidi meant every word. Logic tried to hijack Synna, pushing common sense into the fray and losing miserably.

Heidi gathered up the cards.

"Give me a break," a male voice said behind them, and Synna about jumped two feet.

Tyler came around the side of the table.

"This stuff is garbage," he said as he reached for Synna's arm. "Come on, let's dance."

"It's not garbage." Heidi's objection seemed to have no influence on Tyler at all.

Synna considered objecting, then she stood and allowed Tyler to urge her away. She waved at Heidi. "See you later."

Tyler brought her into his arms right away and tucked against his body.

Sweet and sultry, the tune pulsed against her ears as the night wore onward. She didn't want to be here in this man's arms.

"Hey, what's wrong?" Tyler's frown held serious questions.

"Everything is fine."

His arms tightened until his body slid against her breasts, his hips nudged close. She shifted back from him, her hands on his shoulders, but little else touching. A couple bumped into them and sent her closer to him again. To her horror, his cock grew hard against her stomach. Curls of revulsion nauseated her. She dared glance up at him.

A satisfied grin eased across his face, and she almost yanked out of his arms right then. She didn't think she could do this. Not if the bastard planned to rub his penis against her.

He leaned forward and tried to kiss her.

Synna jerked back, panic striking her as she stumbled out of his arms. She turned to leave, horrified. She couldn't win this one. Either she let him kiss her and risk becoming a weredemon's bride, or she offended Tyler and the SIA lost the chance to bag him.

His strong hand wrapped around her upper arm, and she gasped in pain. "Hey." His voice sounded petulant. "What are you doing?"

She plastered on a rigid smile. "Let me go, please. You're hurting me. I need some air. It's getting stuffy in here."

When he released her, his eyes glittered. "I'll go with you."

"No, that's okay. I'd like a couple of minutes to myself."

The slightly petulant look on his face gave her the creeps. She felt like as if she was dealing with a little kid. *Remember, he's not a child. He's a dangerous demon. Keep remembering that.*

"I'm getting another drink." His voice faded as he walked away.

Synna's glance flicked to the other side of the room as she headed toward the French doors that would lead outside into the gardens.

Then she caught sight of a man so breathtakingly handsome, her heart stuttered and her mouth popped open on a gasp.

Ian.

Chapter Twelve

ഇ

Ian wore a costume resembling a warrior of old. A dark green tunic, intricately decorated with a gold Celtic design, covered his broad chest. A brown velvet cape enveloped his shoulders, and tall black boots reached up to his knees. A gleaming silver scabbard embraced an electrical converter sword and attached to his belted waist. His hair tumbled about his shoulders and his beard growth gave him a rugged edge. She swallowed hard, unable to look away.

When had she ever seen a more rugged, masculine and heartrendingly noble man? Tears came to her eyes. She blinked back the moisture, aware her off-kilter oversensitivity came from fear and other emotions she couldn't name. Things had moved so fast in the last few days, she hadn't taken time to absorb everything that happened.

Steady and true, Ian's gaze captured hers as he approached through the crowd. She waited, everything around her taking on stillness. All her concentration pinpointed on the drop-dead gorgeous man walking her way. A thrill rolled over her as if she'd longed for his kiss for ages, as if he'd returned from a hard battle where she'd feared for his safety. She possessed the anticipation of touch, of taste, of mouth-to-mouth. Fresh feelings arose, and drove Synna to yearn, to want Ian with fervor greater than before.

168

Tyler cleared his throat as he reappeared by her side, but she barely heard him. When Ian stopped close in front of her, she looked into his eyes and smiled.

She drew in a deep breath, trying in vain to control the fluttering in her heart and that trembling sensation in her stomach. "Ian. It's great to see you."

She sensed rather than saw Tyler's displeasure.

Ian nodded to them both, then did a chivalrous bow. His big hand encompassed hers as he brought her fingers to his lips. He pressed a full kiss to the back of her hand, his touch caressing. Heat tingled and raced from the single touch of his lips to her. Warmth surged into her body as physical and mental attraction swamped her. If she'd thought one night of sex and that quickie at work would satisfy her need for him, she'd been mistaken. Ian's gaze burned hot, and the heat inside her built as if he'd done far more than kiss her hand.

Tyler moved closer to her, and Synna bothered to look up at him. A cold light flickered in his eyes, and right then she knew she'd pushed him a little far.

Heidi chose to appear at that moment, and she sidled up to Ian, her smile saccharine and transparent in every way. Synna watched the woman's approach and Ian's response with double interest.

"Mr. Frasier?" Heidi's dark gaze glittered with intent, her smile warmer than necessary as she pressed close to him. "Your costume is exquisite. You look like the guy in that movie—"

"Aragorn," Ian said with a self-effacing grin. "I don't see the resemblance, personally."

Heidi blinked rapidly, and Synna's disbelief went up another notch. Unbelievable.

Heidi slid one hand down the front of his leather vest, her hand looking small against his broad chest. "Oh, but you do. Only better. You're more handsome."

Uncertainty and discomfort flashed over his generally unflappable exterior, and Synna smiled. His insecurity came off boyish and appealing. He didn't know it, but he'd fallen right into a trap by making himself even more attractive to Heidi.

And to you.

Few seconds passed before he recovered a confident demeanor. He smiled, a hint of charm mixed with cockiness. "Thanks, Heidi. You're a gypsy?"

Heidi touched his arm again. "Absolutely." She turned in a circle. "I thought it was pretty sexy."

When Ian's gaze lingered on the woman's cleavage a little longer than she liked, Synna felt jealousy stir like a noxious soup inside her.

No. Don't do this. Now is not the time to let the green-eyed beast take over. Keep on your toes.

Heidi winked at Synna, as if she knew a secret. "Are you dancing tonight, Ian?"

He nodded. "Yes."

Ian tossed a grin at Synna and allowed Heidi to take his arm and lead him away to dance. Synna's stomach lurched.

Tyler walked toward the punch bowl and retrieved a couple of glasses for them. When he returned, he handed her a glass.

She eyed the drink with suspicion. "It's nonalcoholic, right?"

"Yep." He lifted one dark eyebrow. "You got something against spiked punch?"

"Of course not, but tonight I'd like to be totally sober."

She gave the drink a tentative sip. Sure enough, nothing unusual in it. In fact, whoever had made the citrus punch assured the flavor wasn't overwhelmed by sugar. She took another sip before a horrible idea formed. Would Tyler drug her? How could she know? Concerned, she made a face. "I don't know about this punch. A little sour for me."

A small table not far away held several empty punch cups. She put hers down.

"You don't like it?" An almost hurt expression crossed is face.

For a weredemon this guy played the spoiled syndrome a mile wide. "Like I said, it's a little too sour for me."

Silence lengthened between them until she decided to engage him in conversation.

"So, Tyler. Tell me more about your family."

He launched into a full-fledged explanation, and soon she found her thoughts drifting elsewhere as she caught a glance of Heidi and Ian dancing to a fast song.

Admiration overran the jealousy hovering in the background. Even with the burden of a heavy costume, Ian's hips moved, his body found rhythm. A flush burned her face and her body heated. His charisma and sexuality mesmerized her. Heidi looked enthralled. And, damn her, she looked fantastic undulating in a sensual, dramatic synchronicity that fit the music perfectly. Synna caught Tyler's disapproving glance as he stared at the couple.

"You're certainly interested in *them*," Tyler said.

"What?"

"You're jealous of her. Why? You top her in looks any day."

"Well...I-I don't know about that."

His eyes sparkled with unusual intelligence. Maybe she hadn't given him enough credit.

"You're beautiful, Synna." He put his punch on a table and moved closer to her. "I think you need someone to remind you."

She almost took a step back. "That's sweet of you."

He gave her an indulgent smile. "No, it's the truth."

Flattery wouldn't get this man anywhere, though she heard sincerity in his voice. Could it be this weredemon felt genuine admiration?

Oh great, Synna. That's something you could tell your grandchildren one day. A weredemon liked you.

"Come out on the patio and we can talk," he said.

Oh no. No. That wouldn't do.

"How about another dance?" she said and headed for the dance floor as a new song started. Maybe if she kept him distracted with dancing, he'd stop trying to kiss her.

She allowed the weredemon to bring her into a fast dance, although her voluminous brown costume made it difficult. The pace brought up her heart rate, and then she realized how thirsty she'd become. She insisted on stopping for a glass of water, but once she'd gulped it down, Tyler urged her into another fast dance and then two more slow dances.

She started to feel a little strange a few moments later, as if her head was unattached and floating. "Tyler, I've got to take a break. I need to go to the ladies' room."

"All right."

Right on cue, as if she'd set it up, Heidi strode up and snagged Tyler by the arm. "So did you get the ten dollars? I know you want your fortune read."

Tyler's face went blank. "Uh—"

"Come on."

"But—"

"No buts. Let's get to it."

Heidi dragged him off, and as Heidi turned her head to glance back at Synna, she winked.

What on earth? Is that supposed to be some sort of signal?

It didn't matter. She grabbed another glass of water and downed it, but it didn't make her feel any better.

Before she headed to the ladies' room, she surveyed the vast room and didn't see a sign of Ian. Disappointment made her pause, and she glanced around again. Damn, she hated this. How could she ever complete this assignment if she couldn't keep it together long enough to help Ian capture Tyler?

After she went into the restroom, patted cold water on her hot face, and refurbished her makeup, she felt a little better. Getting away from Tyler refreshed her body a thousandfold. She didn't feel completely herself, but at least she didn't have the sensation she might fall on her face any minute.

Dim lighting in the hallway gave it a rosy glow, a weird cozy ambience of intimacy. She'd just reached an open door to one suite and realized it hadn't been open and dark before. An arm reached out and grabbed her. Before she could squeak, the arm yanked her up against a steel-hard body. The light went on and the door slammed and locked.

"What—?!"

"Shh. It's me."

Ian's arm tightened around her waist and brought her up against his rock-solid body, and she sagged in relief. "What are you doing? You scared the crap out of me."

"I saw Tyler sniffing around the entrance to the suites, and I needed to see you before he monopolizes your time again." He gazed down at her with a cross between exasperation and concern. "Are you all right?"

She sighed. "I am now."

His searching gaze took her in, and she did the same with him. Sensual languor overtook her senses as she looked at his rugged form. "God, you look just like..."

His cocky smile ruined the brooding and dangerous effect a little. "You were saying?"

"You *do* look like a blond version of Aragorn in *Lord of the Rings*."

He laughed, throwing back his head and letting loose.

Without trying to hide it, she allowed her gaze to do the same foray over his person that she'd done earlier. Glossy, thick hair shone with red highlights mixed with golden blond. Rugged and masculine, his face seemed carved from granite. Agelessness surrounded him, yet he seemed from the past, a warrior awaiting the pleasure of his lover. A soldier willing to do whatever it took to keep his woman safe.

A shivery thrill darted through her stomach and settled straight between her legs. She licked her lips in appreciation.

His stance, shoulders back and feet planted firmly, showed defiance and unparallel strength mixed with determination. Nothing got past this man. As she took a chance and gazed into his eyes, she saw genuine concern that asked for her understanding and stirred her soul. She'd never seen him look more gorgeous, stronger or more invincible. Here was a man who would always enduringly save the day. An ache started in her heart. But would he deepen that caring? Would he ever feel for Synna the way she felt for him?

"Come on, you're not mad at me," he said.

She slipped her arms around his shoulders and relaxed a little, feeling safe in his arms. "No, I'm not mad. I'm flummoxed."

He laughed again. "Flummoxed. Now that's a word you don't hear every day."

When Synna frowned and didn't respond, he traced his fingers along her jaw.

Fine shivers racked her frame.

"You look flushed. Sure you're all right?" he asked.

"I felt a little strange after dancing with him for a while."

"Strange?" The word came out sharp. "How?"

"Overheated from doing too many dances in this wench outfit."

His mouth turned up at one corner, a flash of amusement in his eyes. He eased her back a little until he could see the front of the dress.

"I like your dress. I would have told you earlier if demon boy hadn't been standing there. I like the low-cut bodice."

He nuzzled her neck. As his lips lingered, a strong, blissful shudder moved through her body.

"I've been watching you dance with him," Ian said, his voice husky with concern. "I don't like it. Damn it, I want you for my own."

His tongue lapped her earlobe, and she gasped at the tingling pleasure. His touch obliterated all her worries about this assignment and the party. Even the room, which she'd barely noticed as a deluxe accommodation with four-poster king-sized bed, a living area, a kitchenette and a whirlpool spa, ceased to exist for her. Only his arms, his touch, his heat, his breath meant anything. She neither saw nor felt anything but Ian.

He worked his way down, kissing the hollow of her neck. His fingers caressed and pressed along her hips, searching for her body beneath layers of restricting fabric. Her small purse fell to the floor.

"I saw you in this dress," he whispered, "and I felt like my throat was closing up. You're so damned sexy."

"Ian." A tremulous breath parted her lips and unexpected tears came to her eyes. What could she say when her heart pounded and her breathing quickened to a furious pace?

She slipped her fingers through his hair as it brushed against her breasts.

His gaze burned with an intensity she'd never seen before.

"You're not jealous of Tyler?" she asked, incredulous.

"Hell, no." His voice roughened. "I'm...hell, yes. I'm jealous, and I'm worried about your safety, and when you told me about how you felt in his arms—fuck it."

He kissed her.

Chapter Thirteen

ഔ

Ian skipped preliminary tastes. A full lip-lock with no pretenses heated her straight to the core.

His lips tasted hers with relentless brushes of lip against lip, an assertive kiss that claimed at the same time it gave. Twisting from side to side, his mouth asked her for full response. Warm and searching, his kiss drew her into a fantasy world. Shivering in fine ecstasy, she undulated and pressed her hips against his. Passion exploded like dynamite, and she wanted him inside her with a relentless, hungry ache.

Sweeping her tongue over his lips, she asked for his surrender and he gave it. His mouth opened and her tongue dipped inside. With a low growl, he took the kiss from another angle, and plunged his tongue into her mouth. Taken, she allowed his dominance, savoring the male, the savage need coursing through him. His tongue rubbed relentlessly over hers, mimicking a deep sexual cadence that screamed cock into pussy.

Warmth pulsed through her nipples and they tightened into pinpoints while her pussy flooded with heated need. She clenched her vaginal muscles, dying to have him inside her this minute. Wet and aching, her body demanded fulfillment with frantic desires.

Must have him.

Must have him now, now, now.

He rapidly bunched her skirts up in back. He slipped inside the back of her g-string panties and cupped her naked ass.

She gasped into his mouth. Keeping one hand on her ass, squeezing and kneading, he reached up and eased her dress off her shoulders. He tugged until the bodice sagged down to her waist. With a quick movement she barely felt, her strapless bra sprang open in the back. Ian never stopped kissing her, and the sensation of tongue against tongue, his hand caressing her ass cheek, and one hand cupping her swollen breast about made her come there and then. They hurled along a path of no return and she craved it.

Ian groaned into her mouth as he lightly gripped her nipple and pinched. She moaned softly and tore her mouth from his, out of breath, panting, aching. With a steady, soft motion of his fingers, he tugged her nipple with feather-soft touches. A steady throbbing began high inside her as her body prepared for the first thrust of his cock.

Angling her hips toward his, she undulated, a motion she knew would drive him wild. If he could torment her into a first-class meltdown, she could make him frantic for her.

"Sweetheart," he murmured against her breast, the rasping deep sound pleading and almost agonized.

Tightly, her throat aching from sensual overload, she whispered, "Ian."

"Now."

"Yes. Now."

One nipple he pleasured under his constant touch, the other he tongued. One lick. Two. Then a deep, steady sucking she thought would send her into a screaming orgasm. His hand kneaded her ass, then his fingers slipped between her butt cheeks and teased the tight rosette.

"Oh shit!" Her gasp came out loudly. "Oh my God."

He stopped sucking her nipple and straightened. His hot breath gusted over her ear. "I'm not finished with you, Synna. You've been driving me insane all evening, and I'll be damned if we're leaving this room before you know you're mine."

His possessive words shocked and delighted her. She once imagined being crazed like this, asked to give herself in unrestrained ways. Yet she'd never believed it would happen or that she'd want it with a fierceness beyond anything she could conjure in her wildest fantasies. In that moment, she knew the truth.

She wanted his cock in her. In every way, in every position, in all the ways a man could take a woman.

She would never want another man the way she desired Ian Frasier.

He licked her earlobe, his words rough and packed with desperation. "I've got to have you."

Like a match to kindling, her desire exploded into full flower.

He slid down her body and crawled under her skirts. She laughed, shaky and breathless. "What are you doing?"

"Son of a bitch," he breathed. "Crotchless. These panties are fucking crotchless."

He took a moment to push her skirts aside so he could look up at her and smile with pure male pleasure. "Have you had these panties for long?"

"Since this morning." She blushed, heat filling her face. "I bought them this morning at a boutique, along with the garter belt and stockings."

"I love it. At this rate you're going to make me come in my pants."

He burrowed under her skirts again. He spread her legs wider. With his fingers and thumbs, he pressed her pussy lips open. She moaned softly, knowing what he would do next and wanting it so much she almost yelled at him to do it.

He blew on her clit, and sweet, tight pleasure tingled through her, aching high inside her.

Warm, hot tongue swept over her clit and she almost collapsed as her thighs shivered. She eased back against the door behind her and spread her thighs further apart. Another lick over her labia, first one side, then the other. Heat burst, shocking her as the tiny orgasm lit her from the inside out. She moaned, unable to keep the sound from leaving her throat. She didn't care if anyone knew she was in here getting her brains fucked out. Her heart wanted more with Ian, more love, more excitement, more life. She couldn't think beyond the hot, unbelievable sensation of his tongue relentlessly tasting between her legs. His tongue pushed and entered her pussy, thrusting and retreating in a relentless beat like cock into pussy. She writhed in his hold, the feelings overwhelming. Two fingers eased into her, pushing up, up until she gasped.

"Ian. Oh my God."

She couldn't breathe, caught up in the tremendous sensation of his fingers pushing in and out, fucking her with steady, slow strokes while his tongue fluttered over her clit, then took long, leisurely laps.

He stopped.

Ian crawled out from under her skirts, and she took a good look at the man who tortured her with sensual pleasure. His eyes gleamed with heated awareness, an animal quality that thrilled at the same time it frightened her in the way every male could scare a woman with his mating lust. His nostrils flared, his lips wet with her juices. He licked his lips and his eyes closed as he heaved a deep breath. His cock pushed against his breeches.

"Please, don't stop," she said, not caring that she begged.

A cocky smile moved over his lips. "A nuke could go off now and nothing would keep me from you."

Tears surged into her eyes, happiness flooding her heart.

He stripped off his clothing, tossing the garments onto the chair until all he wore were his breeches and boots. He removed his belt and sword and placed them carefully on top of his clothes. His naked chest, powerful, his arms bulging with muscle, he leaned his hands against the door behind her and caged her in.

"Turn around, sweetheart."

She turned and pressed against the door, tucked between his arms. He leaned down and helped her remove her flats. She kicked them aside. His hands lingered on her stockings, held up by the garter belt.

"God, fucking stockings. These make me so hot."

Pleased, she laughed softy. "Everything you could want."

She felt him working to undo the breeches. She wanted his naked cock inside her so much she almost begged him to take her. She didn't have long to wait. His broad cock head parted her pussy lips.

"Oh shit." His voice turned hoarse.

With one steady, smooth thrust, he eased inside her from behind.

Her breath caught.

"Too much?"

Her pussy lips swelled so much with arousal he felt huge. "More."

He pulled back, then pushed, inching inside increment by increment.

Then with one plunge, he shoved his entire cock straight up into her pussy.

"Ian." Her word came out strangled as shocking pleasure pierced her.

Ian's cock stretched her to capacity, the tip nudging against her womb. Tonight he felt even larger, the slightest movement inside her causing prickles of pleasure so hot, she thought she would come immediately.

If he moved just a little she would—

He moved his hips ever so slightly.

Her pussy throbbed from down deep, straight from her cervix to where his groin hair meshed with hers.

Her fingers pressed into the door, her eyes opening widely and staring at nothing. "Ian. Oh God, oh God, oh, oh—"

He moved in a subtle motion that brushed up against that spot deep inside her. She moaned, this time low and fervent, her need so explosive she didn't think she could stand another moment.

He leaned into her and pushed until she realized there was more, that he hadn't thrust all the way. She shivered, her whole body shuddering as that final inch took her.

She wouldn't survive. Synna felt like her whole body would come to pieces, rendering her helpless.

That exposure freed her.

Ian slipped his hand up under her skirts in front and found her clit. His fingers feathered over the hard nub and he stirred his hips against her so his cock thrust with tiny pulses, gently stroking against her walls.

Heat deep in her pussy burned with mind-melting pleasure and broke her apart. She muffled her scream as the orgasm erupted. Her walls rippled around his cock as he kept the motion going, a gentle, exquisitely beautiful thrusting as he barely moved inside her.

He fingered her clit, clasping it between his thumb and index finger and strumming in maddening rhythm. The infinitesimal fucking was slow and excruciating. She wanted to scream for him to move harder, faster, fuck her into the next century until she couldn't stand.

No.

He kept up the slow motion, his fingers relentless on her clit. Seconds later he took his fingers, slick with her juices, and his thumb teased her anus. She jerked, the tickling sensation too good to be borne. He tucked his thumb into her anus until he sank all the way.

"Ian, oh my God."

"Like it?"

"Like it? I think I'm going to die."

Leaning in to whisper in her ear, his hips still stirring against her in a steady fucking, he said softly, "You're so hot. So damned hot. Tonight, when we are together again and you're in my arms, I'm going to fuck your ass again."

She could only gasp one word as his erotic suggestion sizzled along her veins. "Yes."

She'd never felt anything so incredible in her life. Not even last night's loving came close.

Ian groaned like a man stretched on a rack. "Oh shit, this is fucking incredible."

"Please." Her whimper set him off.

He drew back and thrust hard. Keeping his thumb deep in her ass, he started a jackhammer motion and plowed into her hard. She almost shrieked at the incredible arousal as his cock rubbed back and forth against a spot high inside her that felt so incredible she gasped for breath. Feeling lightheaded, she leaned against the door as he thrust, his growls and grunts fueling her desire.

Then he eased back and she almost screamed for him to continue.

He removed his thumb from her ass, gripped her hips, and fucked her so relentlessly the motion moved her against the door. Each tremendous thrust pounded into her pussy until she heard the slap of skin against skin and the wet noises as their bodies came together.

Waves of heat blistered her, causing her pussy to clench and release in tight ripples on the cock moving inside her. She moaned loudly, mindless as the world came apart at the seams.

With one last thrust, he jerked against her and a low moan left this throat as his entire body tensed and shivered against her.

His harsh breath rasped against her ear, his big body wrapping around hers. As his arms held her close, tears came to her eyes one more time. His heat, hardness and tenderness enveloped her heart, and stunned her.

Shaking down to the core, Ian brushed the hair away from Synna's neck and kissed her nape. God, she smelled delicious. He wanted to go on, and the way his cock hardened again as he rested inside her, he knew he could take her again in short order. He slowly eased out of her.

He headed for the suite bathroom. "Don't go away."

He glanced in the mirror and grimaced. He was a fucking mess. Like a college boy who'd just tumbled with a girl for the first time.

Maybe because he did feel different. He'd been ravenous, eager to get inside her and put his imprint on her. His desire to possess had driven him to take her hard and fast, their joining an almost animalistic fervor.

He'd wanted to mark himself on her body and soul so that no matter where or how that scumbucket demon touched her, she would never forget how it felt to be loved by a man who cared about her.

He left the bathroom, and as she passed him on the way to use the facilities, he made sure to throw her a warm smile.

Unease rippled through him when she didn't speak, and her smile looked lukewarm at best.

Shit. He'd experienced the best meltdown sex of his life, and she appeared almost unaffected. He knew she'd loved what they did. She shook him up, broke him down, and made him whole.

He donned his costume, sword, and took a moment to do a half-assed job of combing his fingers through his hair.

Hell, if he was supposed to look like Aragorn in *Lord of the Rings*, his hair didn't have to look put together. He grinned into the mirror above the long chest of drawers. He didn't give a prick about who he might resemble in some superficial way. But if it turned Synna on, he'd comply with the fantasy. He'd wear a friggin' clown suit if it would get her off.

Remembering his first glance at her this evening stirred his protective instincts. The dark brown dress, a cross between a nondescript wench and beguiling temptress had about brought him to his knees. The low bodice exposed the top curves of her breasts. She had nice-sized breasts, not too large or too small, and the lace-up front on the dress framed them to perfection. The dress cut in at her slim waist and flared over her hips in yards of fabric. Three-quarter sleeves contoured down to her elbows and ended in a froth of lace.

He closed his eyes and almost groaned. He couldn't afford to get another hard-on. *Lay off the fantasy, Frasier. She needs to get back to work, and so do you. Just because you lost all control…*

Yeah, he could admit it. Synna MacDell rendered him defenseless. He didn't like it, didn't want it, yet he couldn't resist the way she made him feel.

Wanted. Cared for.

Synna made him a new man.

She left the bathroom, hair combed and looking so damned silky he wanted to muss it up again. He could tell she had repaired her makeup as well. She smiled as she crossed the room. She leaned down to pick up her purse. "I'm a mess."

"We both are."

"Yeah, but I look like I've had sex. You look like...like you've been through a minor battle."

He laughed. "Thanks."

She waved one hand in dismissal. "No, I didn't mean that as an insult. You look a little tousled, but that's a good thing. Me...I just looked fucked."

He chuckled again and reached for her, but she danced away.

"Uh, uh, uh. Tyler is going to wonder what happened to me."

At the mention of the demon prick, Ian's anger gauge went up to the red zone. "So?"

"He'll get suspicious, don't you think?"

Unable to keep his hands off her entirely, he cupped her face and felt the delicate, soft flesh. "Remember, he can't read our minds."

"Right."

Her breathy voice feathered along his senses like a touch. His cock twitched. "Damn."

She frowned as he released her. "What's wrong?"

"You're right." He kissed her softly. "You'd better get out of here before I push you skirts up and get between your legs again."

Her cheeks went a pretty pink, her eyes flashing. "Ian. You're so..."

"Yeah?"

The flush in her face deepened. "Naughty."

A grin parted his lips, and he turned her around and marched her to the door. "Later tonight you're going to find out how bad I can be."

"There's more?" She threw a teasing look over her shoulder, hands on her hips.

"Count on it, sweetheart."

She tossed him another knee-weakening smile and started to leave. He grabbed her hand and turned her back to him.

"Hey, you know what?" He caressed the side of her face, then kissed her lips again in a slow, agonizing taste.

"What?" she gasped out when he let her up for air.

"You haven't been stuttering lately."

She smiled. "Maybe it's the sex."

He answered her grin. "Hell, I hope so."

With that parting shot, he let her go and she slipped into the corridor. He allowed the door to click shut, and he stayed in the room for several more heartbeats before he edged open the door and looked both ways. No one lingered in the hallway. SIA didn't monitor this area, determined to give VIPs some privacy. He wouldn't have to worry about anyone with surveillance spying the liaison he'd had with Synna.

Gratified, he moved down the hall toward the party.

* * * * *

Self-consciousness hit Synna on the way back to the party. She probably looked like she'd been yanked through a keyhole backward. More than that, she didn't feel in control. While in the bathroom a moment ago, she'd combed her hair and reapplied her lipstick. Yet she didn't have her senses in order. How could she after a bone-melting encounter with Ian? Turning on her heel, she headed toward the ladies' room she'd spied nearby. She slipped into the restroom one more time, determined to double check out her attire and make sure she didn't look like she'd just rolled in the hay.

While making love with Ian felt wonderful, they'd jeopardized this entire mission by having sex while the party went on. Yep, she must be crazy and Ian even nuttier for allowing hormones to overcome common sense.

Smelling baby powder fresh, the restroom gleamed with highly polished sinks, flattering lighting, and amenities like hand-milled soap, designer fragrances and plenty of cushiony chairs for those who might feel a touch of the vapors. If she could pass out and leave the rest of this night behind wouldn't that be nice? Then again, she didn't want her time with Ian to be a fantasy. Her heart clenched with unhappiness at the idea of never making love with Ian.

Once this weredemon thing is over, that may be exactly what happens. What he said about making love to you may not be the truth. Dorky had told her the truth about having sex to make certain the weredemon couldn't harm her. That didn't mean she meant any more to Ian than a good lay.

Men could lie and they had fibbed to her before. What made Ian any different?

Old doubts assailed her with cruel teeth and even worse memories. She knew women and men made the same mistakes constantly in relationships. Patterns were common and caused many a breakup. She scrubbed her hands over her face. Did she make the same gaffe with Ian that she'd made with the other two men?

She glanced in the mirror and grimaced at what she hadn't noticed before. One of her cheeks looked a little red, and so did her neck. Damn, she had beard burn.

Everyone will know what that's all about.

She sighed. Her body still hummed with lingering pleasure. Ian had taken her to towering heights, and the adrenaline wouldn't leave her anytime soon. But she had to get with the program before Tyler gave up on her and tried to seduce an unsuspecting woman.

The success of this mission depended on her.

The door swung open and Heidi walked inside. "Hey, there you are. Everyone was beginning to wonder. You just disappeared."

Heidi's gypsy costume looked a little rumpled and her eyes looked a little funny—

Heidi's hand flashed out and clamped around Synna's throat. Stunned, Synna started and grabbed Heidi's wrist.

"What—?" Synna managed to choke out.

Before Synna could move or manage another word, the world went black.

Chapter Fourteen

෧

Darkness cloaked Synna, but awareness trickled in drop by drop. A dull pain thudded in the middle of her forehead, and her throat ached. She swallowed with difficulty. Weak and foggy, she didn't move. She heard the slow trickle of water, the hard, uneven surface under her back. She breathed in deeply and caught a whiff of fresh air. Thank God. An ache rolled through her body. The floor or whatever she lay on felt hard as hell. She groaned in soreness and frustration.

She sat bolt upright, her eyes snapping open as she remembered.

Heidi.

The bitch.

Pain stabbed through her forehead at the abrupt movement, but she ignored it as anger roared up inside her. Why had Heidi attacked her? In a fit of jealousy over Ian? It didn't seem likely. Bewildered, she sat still while she tried to clear her thoughts from an insistent fog and a dull throbbing in her skull. How had Heidi overpowered her so easily? Details were a little fuzzy, but Synna remembered the excruciating grip on her neck, and the blackness that quickly followed. Fear edged around the confusion. She needed to escape from here—wherever here was.

Ian. He would notice her absence and look for her. She knew that without doubt.

Dim light filtered around a crack in a doorway. She made it to her hands and knees and crawled toward the door. Under her hands, the floor felt like lumpy stone and not the surface she expected. Nope. Not in the Adora. At least not one of the suites.

Not good.

A cellar or storeroom, perhaps?

Weariness and the nagging headache tried to muddle her brain. Feeling like hell, but realizing she couldn't stay like this, she made the decision to rise to her feet.

She wavered and then paused until dizziness passed. Unsteady, she walked to the doorway and pressed her hands against the surface. Rough wood greeted her touch.

How could Heidi sneak her out of the Adora without someone seeing her? Confused but determined, she fumbled for the doorknob. She turned the cold metal knob and it didn't budge. *Damn!*

Irritated, she pounded on the door with the flats of her hands. "Hey! Hey! Is anyone out there? Help! Help!"

"I wouldn't do that if I was you."

Synna jumped, her heart climbing into her throat and almost choking her. She whirled around, staring into the darkness.

The soft laugh purred, a beguiling feminine voice she knew.

"Heidi," Synna said.

Heidi laughed again. "Yes. Too bad you can't see in the dark. You'd realize how ridiculous you look in that wench costume. I thought I told you not to wear it."

Dumbfounded, Synna stared into the pitch black. "You've got to be kidding? Is that what this is all about? Me wearing a costume?"

"It's all about saving Tyler from you."

"That's ridiculous. I'm not going to hurt him."

"Yes, you are."

She heard a snapping noise and glaring light illuminated the room. Squinting against the light, Synna put her hands over her eyes. Another sharp pain echoed through her skull and she moaned softly. God that hurt.

"Don't play sick with me." Heidi's voice held little emotion. "I know you're tougher than you look."

Anger curled through Synna, and she lowered her hands and squinted into the harsh light. "Gee, thanks."

Heidi glowered, her features carved in harsh dislike. Synna felt the other woman's determination and hatred slice through her like a knife.

Synna glanced around. She stood in the middle of a primitive room about forty feet by forty feet. In the darkness, it had felt much smaller.

Cluttered with boxes and other refuse, it appeared to be an abandoned storage area. The room was windowless, and the single bulb illuminated the dirty stone floor and dingy gray stone walls.

"W-where are we?" Synna asked.

"Somewhere you can't escape."

"How did we get here?"

Heidi wore the same smug smile she'd worn in the restroom earlier. "I transported us."

"Transported?" Synna felt dumb as a box of rocks, and the fuzziness in her head didn't help. She was vaguely surprised that fear hadn't crept into her psyche yet. That in itself didn't make sense.

Heidi came closer, and her walk looked different and not quite as steady. "Did you really think you could hurt Tyler? I know you think he's an idiot, but he's not."

"I never said he was an idiot. I didn't know you cared for him so much."

"He's my brother, of course I care."

"What?"

"My brother, you moron."

Synna's legs didn't feel steady. She moved at a snail's crawl until she reached a barren twin-sized mattress on a metal frame sitting against one wall. She sank down on the cushioning with a soft moan as her body ached from head to toe. Instead of feeling better, she'd started to feel worse.

Synna shook her head. "T-Tyler is your brother?"

Heidi's eyes narrowed and flashed with annoyance. A strange golden light sparked inside. "God, I never realized how stupid you really are. He's a weredemon."

"I know that already." Understanding came to Synna in a slow wave. "Wait. So are you."

"Right." Heidi laughed, and this time the slow chuckle didn't sound like the Heidi Synna had known. "Finally you get it."

Synna didn't get it. At least not totally. She sagged back against the wall and shivered. Cold crept into her bones like a sickness. The longer she stayed in this damp, chilly place, the worse she felt. She couldn't even generate much emotion. Everything felt stunted and unreal.

"What do you want from me?" Synna asked.

Heidi stayed glued to one spot on the floor. "Your energy force. All humans have a life force. A very strong one."

Fear managed to trickle around the increasing lethargy in Synna's body. "Why do you want mine? What have I ever done to you?"

"When I read the cards tonight they revealed your plan to me."

Ah, damn. The tarot deck. "You weren't really reading my future, you were reading your own."

Heidi sauntered toward her, and Synna tightened her muscles in preparation in case she needed to fight. Of course, if she fought, she had a horrible feeling she might lose. If her heart hadn't been pounding ten thousand beats a minute, Synna thought she might actually find this conversation intriguing.

"I never would have guessed in a million years that you were a demon," Synna said.

Heidi's lips actually curled. "A weredemon. There's a difference."

"Right."

"What are you planning to do?"

"I think I need a new body. This one is getting a little tiresome." Heidi approached, and Synna understood if she didn't act soon, she'd be a goner in a heartbeat.

Synna swallowed hard. "Tell me more about weredemons. I'd like to know how they operate. If I'm going to die, at least I'd like to know why."

Heidi stood over her, a devilish smile on her face and a red glow covering her eyes. "It's simple. The weredemon are on a path to crush humankind. We will inherit the earth."

"That doesn't tell me much. If you're going to possess my body, the least you can do is explain how all this weredemon crap started."

Confusion played over Heidi's face. "You think I'm going to take time to explain it to you? Are you insane?"

"It's the least you can do." Synna crossed her arms and played her cards. "How long have you lived in that body? Or have you always been Heidi?"

"I've been in Heidi's body two years. I met her at a lesbian club. When she went to her room, that's when I kissed her and possessed her body."

"And the body you were in before? What happened to them?"

"I'd lived in old Elsa Crammer for too damned long."

"Old?"

"Yeah. She was close to forty-five."

"Uh-huh." Synna kept the inflection on the last sentence. "Yep, forty-five is absolutely ancient."

"Don't be sarcastic. I didn't want to be in that woman's body anymore. I want to be young constantly."

"You're not much different from the majority of people." Synna couldn't help a little snort of laughter. "That's pretty funny, if you think about it. It makes you more human."

"I am partly human, you twit." Heidi loomed over her, her cruelty running clear in her eyes and the tension rolling off her in waves.

"Okay, so you are part human. How many bodies have you occupied?"

"Twelve."

"My God."

The weredemon shrugged. "The first two were young kids. I tried them out but discovered ten year olds aren't much fun to possess." Heidi chuckled. "No, adults are much more fun."

"So you've been alive how long?"

Heidi started to pace. "Three hundred years."

Although her insides felt like jelly, Synna kept up the banter. "That's a lot of people."

Again, that unconcerned shrug lifted Heidi's shoulders. "So."

Anger eroded Synna's plan to keep the weredemon occupied. "So, you interrupted people's lives. Don't you feel any guilt?"

"The Shadow Realm isn't the same as your world. There is no guilt. We don't understand it. We don't take it on when we possess a human."

"Is that the Shadow Realm you're talking about, or just you?"

The weredemon rounded on her with a growl, and the sound filled the room like a lion's roar. Synna flinched as the loud noise bounced off the walls.

Synna managed to choke out another question. "Where will I be when you possess me?"

The question sounded moronic even to her ears, but she wanted to understand.

Heidi's eyes snapped wide. "Gone. Just absorbed as a part of me. You see, there's something people don't know about weredemons." She stopped, her stance only a foot away from Synna. "With each new possession, a weredemon absorbs their victim's personality. We're like a sponge." Her eyes seemed to glow with the excitement of a kill almost accomplished. "I have a part of everyone I've ever taken within me. It makes me more powerful with each body I absorb. Someday I'll be one of the most powerful weredemons alive. I'll help the cause of the weredemons."

Synna's body shook now as if with fever. "W-what cause?"

"I told you. Domination of the human race. We're more capable. Stronger. You humans are mucking up the entire world."

Fury gave Synna a little more strength. "So you don't feel any remorse that you're going to kill off the human race? What qualifies you to run the earth? You're not even from our dimension."

Heidi threw her head back and laughed. "You've got to be kidding. Why? The human-weredemon hybrid is a wonderful thing. Take consolation in knowing your absorption will help build a newer, stronger race. We can run your so-called dimension a hundred times better than you can. And better yet, we can go back and forth between the dimensions at will, something humans can't do very often, if at all."

Growing dread assaulted Synna. She tried to stand and found her legs still wouldn't hold her. As she sank back onto the cot, her stomach rolled. She put one hand to her stomach and barely stifled a groan. For a sickening second, she gave up. Humiliation for failing rose inside her.

Pain lanced like needles into her heart. She would miss Ian.

No. Agony ran through her at the thought of never seeing him again. She loved him with soul-deep certainty.

Mixed with the knowledge she loved him came a desire to understand one thing.

"Do you want Ian?" Synna asked as the nausea eased.

Walking from one end of the room to the other, Heidi smiled with self-assured arrogance. An ethereal breeze ruffled her colorful costume, lifting the material into a delicate dance on the air. It would be almost beautiful if Heidi weren't so evil.

"Ian's a side benefit. Since I've been in female forms all my lives, I've developed a taste for human sex. Ian won't even know you're dead."

Synna shivered. *Never.* She couldn't let this horrid creature have Ian. "He'll know it's not me."

Heidi sniffed. "Right."

Rage boiled up inside Synna unlike anything she'd felt before. Emotion punched up from her soul with blinding resentment.

She wouldn't allow any stinking weredemon to harm Ian. Then, in what might be her last reckless act on earth, Synna tried standing once more. Her legs held. "You will *not* hurt Ian."

Heidi stopped pacing, her fiery eyes and expression held surprise. "What?"

"You won't have sex with him." Synna took a step toward the weredemon, then another. "Besides, you can't possess me. I've already made love with Ian. Unprotected sex."

Heidi barked out a short laugh. "You think that is going to save you from me. Taking Ian's semen into your body just kept Tyler from taking you as a weredemon bride. It doesn't keep me from possessing your body."

A wave of terror, sudden and almost crippling, made Synna's resolve waver. Then she stiffened her spine and took a deep breath. "Well, then. Fuck you and the horse you rode in on."

Heidi glared, her teeth bared in a snarl as she met Synna halfway across the room.

Synna's pulse drummed in her ears. She came nose-to-nose and glare-to-glare with the weredemon and straightened to her full height. "This is *my* dimension, not yours. I'm not going to let you or any other badass creatures take over. Do you hear me you...you bitch!"

Synna's temper boiled over and she slapped Heidi across the face with a loud crack that resounded in the small room like a rifle shot.

Heidi's eyes went furnace-blast crimson, pupils and irises obscured by a temperature more heinous than hell itself. She sent a huge energy shaft down on Synna, blue spraying from her hands like water from a fountain. Agony seared Synna, lightning-hot. She crumpled to her back and gasped for air. All her nerves felt on fire, the flash of pain almost unbearable.

Heidi's hateful voice continued. "Allow me in and your torment vanishes. You'll never feel pain again."

Synna tried to speak, her throat tight and closed to everything but a pitiful moan. Defeat cloaked her. She couldn't fight. She couldn't think beyond the horrible sensations prickling and dancing through her nerve endings like electricity through wire. Synna struggled with darkness as night tried to envelop her thoughts, to vanquish her forever. Light dimmed, and her heart slowed to a dull thud. Trickling like a small waterfall, her mind asked a question and got no answer. If Heidi took over her body, would Synna die? Simply blink out like a light bulb extinguished?

A growing sense of wellbeing should have given her pause. Instead, she went with it, taken over by the knowledge nothing mattered but giving in to the darkness. Heidi planned to remove her from the picture. What could she do?

Heidi smirked. "That's it. Give into the torpor. Know once I've taken your body, Ian will also be mine."

Synna screamed in her mind, fear and hate bursting forth in a great tide. She screamed and screamed and screamed.

Splintered by Heidi's energy, she took a last breath and gathered enough strength to eject a thought.

I love you, Ian. Please help me.

* * * * *

"Hey, something wrong?" Ben Darrock asked Ian as they stood near the dance area.

Ian scanned the crowd and frantically searched for Synna. Where the hell was she? "Synna should be here."

"Maybe she's talking with Heidi. I don't see her anywhere either."

Pain hit Ian in the solar plexus, and he grimaced as he stepped back against the wall. Something was wrong. Really wrong.

Synna. Oh shit.

Ben reached for Ian's arm. "Are you all right?"

"Tyler's not anywhere in sight either. Come on. We've got to find her. Son of a bitch, I shouldn't have let her out of my sight. If anything's happened to her—"

"Easy. We'll find her." Ben grabbed his shoulder again. "It's better if we split up. I'll head this way." Ben retrieved his I-Doc communications device and spoke into it. "Team Six, we've got an emergency."

Ben took off toward the garden entry double doors. Grateful for the Scot's assistance, Ian's mind ran at high speed as he kicked himself for not keeping her in his sights at all time. *Stupid. Stupid. Stupid.*

Searing worry gripped him, a physical pain like fire in his body. The woman he loved could be in grave danger right now. Wrenching self-recrimination tore a hole in his heart. Scalding emotion drove him. His throat tightened as he jammed down the desire to run through the halls screaming her name. Instead he pulled out his I-Doc. After contacting the other agents assigned to the case tonight, he continued his search.

Frustration mixed with continuing fear as he strode out of the dance area. He made a turn in the long hallway, past the room where he'd made love with Synna tonight.

The door popped open. Ian's right hand went to the hilt of his sword. All his muscles gathered tight for action.

Tyler stepped out of the suite, wide-eyed and startled. "What are you doing here?"

Ian kept his grip on the weapon. He stalked toward the man and gripped him by the collar. He drove him back against the wall near the suite door. Tyler didn't struggle, his eyes frightened.

"Where is she, Hessler? What the fuck did you do with her?"

"Who?" Ian twisted the collar so Tyler's voice came out as a whisper. "If you're talking about Synna—"

"Yeah, I'm talking about Synna. Where is she?" Ian knew he should keep cool, interrogate the suspect rationally. He couldn't, his voice rasping harshly. "I swear to God if you've hurt her, I'll kill you myself."

Tyler's eyes flashed red for a second. "I was looking for her myself. She said she was going to the ladies' room, but that was almost forty-five minutes ago."

Sheer disbelief ran through Ian. "Right. She's been gone that long and you didn't think to look for her before that?"

"Well...I...not exactly. I had other pressing business."

"What kind of business?"

Tyler's gaze shifted right, then left. "It's personal."

"That's bullshit."

Tyler stayed mum, and Ian made a decision. He kept tight hold on the smaller man's collar. "Let's put it this way, Hessler, we know who you are and what you are. I could use this sword on you right now without giving you a chance to redeem yourself."

Tyler's dark brows winged up. "No. You don't understand."

Ian almost growled. "I don't understand? Either you tell me what you've done with Synna, or I'll make sure you're back on the express train to hell."

Tyler's jaw sagged. "You really *do* know what I am."

"You're damned right."

"You wouldn't send me back to the Shadow Realm."

"I not only can, I will. This weapon doesn't play around. It hurts like a son of a bitch. You want to try it on for size?"

"No, no."

"Good. Then tell me where you've taken Synna. If she's hurt in any way, I'll make you sorry you were ever born."

Ben walked up, his I-Doc clutched in his hand and a fierce expression marring his face. "Has he said where she is?"

Ian almost growled the words. "No. Apparently he'd rather I just barbeque his hairy ass right here."

Ben's grin took on an evil bent. "If that doesn't sound like a damned lot of fun. Let's do it."

"No!" Tyler squirmed in Ian's grip, but Ian held tight.

The weredemon's strength gathered under Ian's fingers, and he knew if Tyler wanted to, he could fling Ben and himself away like annoying fleas.

"I'm too fast for you, Tyler. And you don't want Ben to get his hands on you."

Ben grinned. "No, you don't want that."

"If you tell us where she is, and she's unharmed, we'll consider letting you live. In the Shadow Realm."

Tyler's eyes went from crimson to cinnamon in a microsecond, and his breath heaved out. "I don't believe you."

"Tell me what you've done with Synna—" Ian held the sword to the creep's throat, "—or I won't bother with sending you back to the Shadow Realm. I'll just deal with your rotten carcass right here, right now."

"You wouldn't." Tyler's voice squeaked. "You're the good guys. The SIA. You're not supposed to kill weredemons."

Ian snorted. "Where did you hear that bullshit?"

Ben laughed. "Yeah, where did you hear that?"

Tyler gaped, his face pale. "Okay. I'll tell you. It's just not...it's not what you think. I didn't hurt her."

"You put your lips on her, asshole." Ian's anger gripped him, his breathing heavy as he glared at Tyler. "She's mine. Do you hear me, she's mine!"

Tyler's eyes went wide. "Yeah, I hear you."

"Where the fuck is she?" Ian asked, gritting the words through his teeth. "Tell me."

"Heidi is a weredemon, too. She's my sister. We're both three hundred years old, and we've...we've been out of touch for a while. But she found me here. I didn't want her here. I didn't want her mucking everything up like she did the last few lives." Tyler's voice shook. All the demon hell seemed drained from him.

"What are you bloody babbling about?" Ben asked.

"Heidi's my blood sister. But she's taken on different bodies since we were both born in the Shadow Realm. So have I, but I don't hurt nice people. I only take the bodies of mean people. Arrogant, greedy, nasty people."

Ben snorted. "Right. Like I bloody well believe that."

Ian tightened his grip on the weredemon, rage threatening to send his last bit of control into meltdown. "You lying sack of shit. You kissed Synna against her will and you weren't concerned about what she wanted or felt."

"I'm telling the truth! When I realized that Heidi wanted to possess Synna, I decided I had to do something about it. When Heidi possesses another woman, she takes her body. Synna's body won't die, but it won't be the Synna you know anymore."

Ian's heart thumped loudly in his ears as Tyler's words sank in.

Tyler continued, explaining how Heidi planned to murder Synna in cold blood. "I think she plans to take Synna somewhere underground. I don't know where for sure, but Heidi has always liked places underground to do her dirty work."

Ben snapped his fingers. "Maybe the outbuildings behind here. There's a basement in there."

"That's it. That would be a good place for her to take Synna," Tyler said.

Ian's grip tightened on the weredemon's collar. "I swear to God, Tyler Hessler, or whatever your real name is—"

"Adromedus," Tyler whispered. "Adromedus."

"You're a dead demon if you're lying. Dead." Ian glanced at Ben. "Come on. Let's find somewhere to put this piece of shit."

Ben grinned evilly. "Here, let me take him off your hands."

Ian relinquished his grip on the weredemon long enough for Ben to grab him by the collar and march him down the hallway.

"Here, let's put him in here," Ian said as they stopped next to the suite where he'd made love to Synna.

Ian used the key card and let them inside. When they entered, Tyler wrenched around and took a swing at Ben. The haymaker landed on Ben's jaw and knocked him back into a table. He went flying and landed with a hard thud on his back.

Ian growled and lunged at the weredemon with his sword.

Ben surged to his feet and readied his stance to fight, his eyes hot with anger. "Fuck me! That hurt, Hessler. You're going to pay."

Ian flicked the power switch on his sword and took a swing. He sliced Tyler's shoulder and the contact sent a surging shock through the weredemon as it cut his flesh. Tyler gasped and his body trembled as a crackling noise filled the air. Tyler's hair stood on end, his eyes wide as if he was surprised they'd retaliated this way.

Tyler collapsed in a heap on the floor, out cold. The wound on his shoulder closed up immediately.

"Dumb son of a bitch." Ian's chest heaved as he stood over the unconscious creature.

"Nothing says every weredemon is smart. Much as I hate to say it, I don't think he meant to hurt me that much. He could have knocked my head off my shoulders. Literally. Weredemons are immensely strong," Ben said as he rubbed his jaw and winced.

"You okay?"

"I'm great."

"Then let's tie him up and find Synna."

* * * * *

Ian's heart pounded in his chest, his breath heaving as he ran full blast toward the outbuildings. For all the assignments he'd been on abroad as an Alpha Unit soldier, he'd never felt like this. Torn up. His guts churned with a terror he couldn't reason with or force back. *Oh God, it might be too late. Why did I let her out of my sight?*

Ian slid to a stop near the bushes by the storage building where Tyler thought Heidi might be holding Synna. Ian crouched low, his eyes accustomed to the dark, but grateful for the moonlight silvering the night.

Ben's voice came over the I-Doc. "We're coming up on the other side of the buildings. We'll check the back rooms first."

Ian spoke into the device, wanting to leave caution behind and do whatever it took to bring his woman back into his arms. "Heidi isn't going to take her, Ben. I'll kill Heidi first."

"I know," Ben said his voice filled with quiet understanding.

Tyler lay trussed up in the suite. He wouldn't come to for hours, giving the SIA enough time to carry his carcass to the reintroduction chamber within the bowels of the SIA. No one would ever have to worry about him prowling SIA and maybe harassing another woman or trying to possess her for his own.

Ian's heart ached. What would he do if Heidi had already taken Synna's body? What would he do? Rage surged inside him. Nothing mattered but this mission to get her back.

Moonlight bathed the outbuildings in a ghostly glow. Hell, a weredemon didn't need light to see. Ian staked out the front of the building. Sparks suddenly flew from the rooftop.

"Damn it!" He hissed his next words into the I-Doc. "Ben, we've got to get Synna out of there. That weird light around the rooftop is demon glow."

"Demon what?"

"Demon glow. It's used by the weredemons to take a human's soul!"

Pain burned in Ian's chest as furiously as the light dancing off the roof of the outbuilding like St. Elmo's Fire.

"We won't be able to break down the doors if Heidi's locked them," Ben said.

"Then we'll just have to use our weapons." Without hesitation, Ian ran toward the building.

Ian didn't wait. With a surge of strength, he jammed his shoulder against the front door. Wood cracked and the lock came free from the door partway. With a deep growl, he lifted his sword and brought it down on the lock with all his force. Metal clanged and fire danced off the lock as the door flew open. He heard Ben and his team battering the back door. Above him the roof pulsated with a weird rainbow light. He plunged into the room.

Only a couch, two chairs, coffee table and lamps occupied the small bungalow living room. He worked from room to room, into the kitchen, the dining room, and finally the large master bedroom. Nothing.

The back door slammed against the kitchen wall, and he heard Ben cry out his name.

Ian called out acknowledgement and moved into the kitchen at the same time. "She's not in here."

Two of Ben's team members, a young female agent and an older man, followed behind with their swords drawn.

Ian saw the light streaming in great waves from under the basement doorway. Heat radiated from the area. "Oh my God."

"Shit," Ben said, his voice agonized. "No one can survive that."

Ian headed for the basement door. "Synna isn't dead. I'd feel it in my heart. She isn't dead."

"Wait." Ben reached for Ian's arm and missed. "Damn it, you can't go down there."

Ian glared at the Scotsman. "If it was someone you loved, what would you do?"

Ben didn't hesitate, resignation on his face. "Break down the fuckin' door."

"Let's do it," Ian said.

All agents headed for the door.

"Ready?" Ian aimed his sword at the door, hoping the combined electrical heat would work.

Ben's weapon went off at the same time, and intense light melted the doorknob and made a huge hole.

Instantly, the unholy heat emanating from the room ceased and the light diminished.

Ian charged through with Ben and the others close behind. What Ian saw sent pure fury through his blood.

Heidi stood over Synna's body. Synna lay on the floor by a dingy cot, her costume torn, the bottom singed, her hair matted and blood coming from one ear.

At least she wasn't burned.

A glimmer of hope entered Ian's heart.

"Back away from her," Ian said.

Ben and his team aimed their weapons at the weredemon.

Heidi laughed as she turned toward them, the throat sound harsh and manic.

"Step away from her, Heidi," Ben said in echo.

"Why should I?" Her voice sounded guttural, almost mannish. "She's dead and now I'll possess her." Her eyes, a harsh coals-on-fire red, glittered at him with strange intensity and assurance, as if she had all the time in the world. "She's not the same person and soon I'll be her."

Ian brought up his weapon, the pain of knowing his beloved lay dead cleaving his heart so deep he knew he'd never recover. "Take this then, bitch!"

He aimed the weapon at her heart. With lightning speed, her hands lashed out and blue light arched into him with paralyzing punch, catching his breath and holding it prisoner. The force lifted him up and slammed him back into the wall. His weapon sailed across the room out of reach. Ben's weapon went off. Heidi dodged the energy bolt with amazing speed.

"She's dead, you idiot!" Heidi charged Ian. "You belong to me now!"

Ben and his team laid down another stream of blistering heat rounds, but no matter what they did, she moved away effortlessly.

Ian ached from head to toe, but he pulled himself to his feet. Through his dimmed and dizzy vision he thought he saw Synna rise and climb to her feet.

It couldn't be.

Synna rose from the dead and grabbed his weapon from the floor. She aimed at Heidi. Light streamed from the point of the sword and struck Heidi in the middle of the back. A sizzling sound pierced the air, and Heidi's eyes widened as she gasped and shivered.

A thin scream left Heidi's throat, and her skin turned darker brown before it collapsed inward. Ian watched in horrified fascination as she shriveled like a crushed paper bag. One second the weredemon's desiccating form was there, the next, it popped out of view. Only a wisp of smoke remained.

Ian rushed for Synna and gathered her in his arms as her eyelids fluttered and closed. "Synna! Synna!"

The others rushed toward them.

"Come on. We've got to get her to the infirmary," Ben said.

* * * * *

Synna's dreams filled with hellfire and burning waves dancing along the ceiling.

*Why is the ocean on fire? S*he opened her eyes to the most welcome vision in the world.

Ian's head lay propped on his arms on the bed. With his shaggy hair tossed about, she couldn't see his face. Seeing him so near filled her heart with warmth and joy.

With a gasp, he jerked awake and looked at her.

His eyes went sharp and intense. He reached for her hand lying on the pillow. "Thank God. You're awake." He stood and leaned over to kiss her forehead. "You scared the shit out of me."

"It's what I do best, apparently." She laughed softly.

He touched her forehead, and the look in his eyes held amazing tenderness. "How do you feel?"

She smiled. "I feel great. Like nothing happened." She glanced around the cream-walled room and the hospital bed. "Where am I?"

"The local hospital. You were at the infirmary, but we decided you should be here for treatment. They've tested your system to make sure there was no permanent damage. You were out so long because your body was healing. You're free and clear of any weredemon possession. Apparently, my semen actually acted as protection in more than one way. It kept the Demon Glow from destroying you."

Added relief flowed through her in grateful waves. "Tell me what happened. I only remember little bits."

"Rest now." He lifted her hand and kissed her fingers reverently. "You need to take it easy."

"I need to know. What happened to Heidi and Tyler?"

"You killed Heidi. Tyler was sent back to the Shadow Realm."

Shock kept her quiet for a long minute. "I killed Heidi?"

After his explanation, she took a deep breath. She couldn't speak, overwhelmed.

He leaned over and kissed her forehead again. "Are you all right?"

"It's just a lot to take in right now."

"You did a damn fine job defending yourself. Ben and I were struggling."

She saw guilt in his face and squeezed his hand. "Don't you dare blame yourself for what happened. If it hadn't been for you, I'd be dead."

She frowned and he squeezed her hand. The dark circles under his usually sparkling eyes and his overall rough appearance made her wonder. "How long have I been out?"

A heaving sigh left him. "Two days."

"Oh my God. You've been here all that time, haven't you?"

He nodded, his brow creased. "Of course." His eyes shimmered, haunted. "Don't you know by now?"

"Know what?"

His words came soft and reverent. "I love you, Synna."

A gentle smile touched his mouth, and the kindness and love she saw brought tears to her eyes. "And I love you."

He sat on the edge of the bed and drew her up into his arms. As he held her, he buried his face in her hair. "The moment you're well, you and I are taking a long weekend."

She pulled back to look into his handsome face. "Yeah?"

"Oh yeah," he said in a husky whisper.

"Where?"

"Your bed or my bed. I don't care which. But we're locking ourselves in there for a couple of days with provisions."

"Provisions, eh?"

He grinned. "Food. Water. Sex toys."

"Sounds like heaven."

Epilogue
Five days later

⁊ↄ

Synna sighed as Ian's tongue bathed her nipple with a wide, even stroke. They'd spent the last four hours feasting on each other in every way imaginable. They hadn't ventured into the sex toys they'd bought earlier in the week. They had bought condoms, though, and now that the weredemon danger was gone, they used them every time they made love.

Right now all Synna wanted with Ian was raw, hot sex in the most basic man-on-top-of-woman way. They'd fucked in every position they could think of, their lovemaking frenzied. She'd never felt this out of control, and he'd confessed earlier that he'd never made love for this long in his life. They kissed, they hugged, they'd washed up in the shower. Moments later Ian had spread her half-naked out on the kitchen table, his cock hammering between her legs until she screamed out in tortured orgasm.

Now, as he paid homage to her tender breasts and hardening nipples, she thought she couldn't possibly be aroused again.

Boy was she wrong.

Hot shivers rippled over her skin as delight left her mouth in a sigh. "That's wonderful." She smiled up into his eyes, her grin mischievous. "You have to be the world's greatest lover. I've never had that many orgasms in a row in my life."

He reached for another condom and slipped it on, then slowly levered himself over her. "Really?"

"I'm not kidding you. It's—"

His cock plunged, spearing her wet, slick pussy. She gasped, then groaned as he withdrew and thrust. "You were saying?"

Synna could barely form a thought as his cock massaged her walls and set off wild tingles of enjoyment deep inside her.

"My time at SIA ends next week," she managed to say.

"And?"

"Now that I'm leaving the SIA, and everyone on the green earth seems to know about us, what do we do next?"

His hips stirred into gentle motion, so slow and methodical she felt the pleasure building by stages. "I was hoping you'd want to move in with me."

A thrill sent a stirring straight down to her stomach and added to the arousal driving her higher with each stroke.

She felt bolder than she'd ever been in her life. "You want me to move in with you?"

He tilted one eyebrow and his hips ground against hers. His pupils dilated, his breathing coming faster. "There's more room here at my place for both of us. Besides, I've got a state-of-the-art security system."

She frowned. "You think Tyler might try to come back from the Shadow Realm?"

"Not anytime soon, but it's something we'll have to keep on guard for. Does that worry you?"

She tilted her hips up to meet another slow, hot thrust, her thoughts fogging with desire. "Yes. But there's nowhere I'd rather start my new career in art than in this lovely home with you."

He smiled, the curving of his lips tender and reassuring. The pace of his thrusts increased, heating her from the inside out. "Have I told you how much I love you lately?"

"I think a few times just today."

"I'm telling you again," he whispered against her lips, "because I want more."

Pleasure heated along her nerves. Her breathing came faster and her fingers clutched at his shoulders. She wrapped her legs around his hips.

He groaned as the motion brought him deeper. "I know it might seem too soon, but I want you to marry me, Synna."

His question broke her motion. "What?"

Ian peppered her face with kisses and ended with a soul-searching taste. "I don't want just a live-in arrangement. I want you in my life forever. I want you with me through day and night, thick and thin. I love you too much to have anything else."

With a little sob of joy, she kissed him deeply.

He grinned. "Is that a yes?"

"Yes, yes!"

Joy entered his eyes, and he kissed her with a passion she knew would last forever.

Ecstasy speared her entire body as Ian's cock moved between the slick, swollen folds of her pussy and deep inside. Nothing mattered but being with him, taking him with her for this time and for always.

He rode her hard. "God yes!"

Orgasm slammed her. Hot pleasure contracted her muscles over his thrusting cock. As she arched up against him and her entire body shook, she let out a wail.

Ian lay full on her and gathered her closer, his hips pumping furiously. A low, harsh growl left his throat. He buried his face in her throat and shuddered as he climaxed long and hard.

As he settled into her arms, she sighed and held him close. She knew deep within her heart that it would always be like this for them.

"I love you," she whispered. "Now and for always."

About the Author

‰

Suspenseful, erotic, edgy, thrilling, romantic, adventurous. All these words are used to describe award-winning, best-selling novelist Denise A. Agnew's novels. Romantic Times Magazine called her romantic suspense novels *Dangerous Intentions* and *Treacherous Wishes* "top-notch romantic suspense." With paranormal, time travel, romantic comedy, contemporary, historical, erotica, and romantic suspense novels under her belt, she proves her gift for writing about a diverse range of subjects. (Writing tales that scare the reader is her ultimate thrill.)

Denise's inspiration for her novels comes from innumerable sources, but the fact she has lived in Colorado, Hawaii, and the United Kingdom has given her a lifetime of ideas. Her experiences with archaeology have crept into her work, as well as numerous travels throughout England, Ireland, Scotland, and Wales. Denise currently lives in Arizona with her real life hero, her husband.

Denise welcomes comments from readers. You can find her website and email address on her author bio page at www.ellorascave.com.

Why an electronic book?

We live in the Information Age—an exciting time in the history of human civilization in which technology rules supreme and continues to progress in leaps and bounds every minute of every hour of every day. For a multitude of reasons, more and more avid literary fans are opting to purchase e-books instead of paperbacks. The question to those not yet initiated to the world of electronic reading is simply: *why?*

1. *Price*. An electronic title at Ellora's Cave Publishing and Cerridwen Press runs anywhere from 40-75% less than the cover price of the <u>exact same title</u> in paperback format. Why? Cold mathematics. It is less expensive to publish an e-book than it is to publish a paperback, so the savings are passed along to the consumer.

2. *Space*. Running out of room to house your paperback books? That is one worry you will never have with electronic novels. For a low one-time cost, you can purchase a handheld computer designed specifically for e-reading purposes. Many e-readers are larger than the average handheld, giving you plenty of screen room. Better yet, hundreds of titles can be stored within your new library—a single microchip. (Please note that Ellora's Cave and Cerridwen Press does not endorse any specific brands. You can check our website at www.ellorascave.com or

www.cerridwenpress.com for customer recommendations we make available to new consumers.)

3. *Mobility.* Because your new library now consists of only a microchip, your entire cache of books can be taken with you wherever you go.

4. *Personal preferences are accounted for.* Are the words you are currently reading too small? Too large? Too...**ANNOYING**? Paperback books cannot be modified according to personal preferences, but e-books can.

5. *Instant gratification.* Is it the middle of the night and all the bookstores are closed? Are you tired of waiting days—sometimes weeks—for online and offline bookstores to ship the novels you bought? Ellora's Cave Publishing sells instantaneous downloads 24 hours a day, 7 days a week, 365 days a year. Our e-book delivery system is 100% automated, meaning your order is filled as soon as you pay for it.

Those are a few of the top reasons why electronic novels are displacing paperbacks for many an avid reader. As always, Ellora's Cave and Cerridwen Press welcomes your questions and comments. We invite you to email us at service@ellorascave.com, service@cerridwenpress.com or write to us directly at: 1056 Home Ave. Akron OH 44310-3502.